Horace Eaton Walker

Intimations of Heaven and Other Poems

Horace Eaton Walker

Intimations of Heaven and Other Poems

ISBN/EAN: 9783744707879

Printed in Europe, USA, Canada, Australia, Japan

Cover: Foto ©Andreas Hilbeck / pixelio.de

More available books at **www.hansebooks.com**

Intimations of Heaven

INTIMATIONS OF HEAVEN

AND OTHER POEMS

BY

HORACE EATON WALKER

"Ars longa, vita brevis."

CLAREMONT N. H.
GEO. I. PUTNAM CO.
1898

CONTENTS

.

INTIMATIONS OF HEAVEN

*I gathered me also silver and gold, and the peculiar treas-
ure of kings and of the provinces: I gat me men singers and
women singers, and the delights of the sons of men, as musi-
cal instruments, and that of all sorts.*—Ecclesiastes.

1.

Hear: "Vanity of vanities"; but I:
  Have profit in thy labors all thy days,
  And tho' the generations pass, the lays
Of well-spent hours shall sing to thee. The sky
Shall hold the glorious sun. The winds shall dry
  The earth, go to the torrid south; the blaze
  Of suns shall blind: but have a heart and Mays
Will be as lilting birds that once did fly.

For in these days we need the largest hope,
  Since Doubt is mountainous in all our lives;
Many today in horrid darkness grope;
  But I: As bees about their honeyed hives
Let joys flock round thy hearts. Fling doubt and stretch
The portals of thy being, doubting wretch!

II.

And though all streams run to the emerald sea,
    The sea is still unfilled; but may thy heart
    For very gladness be o'erfilled; and art,
And song, and merry-making be to thee
An aureole above thy life: for glee
    Is medicine to every heart. In mart,
    In by-ways, and green lanes, let joys upstart,
And heaven to earth be a reality!

The cup of gladness; drink it to the dregs,
    As some old bibber lost in happiness,
And every nest will have its speckled eggs
    Of new delights. Put on thy wedding dress.
Regain the smiles when love first made thee bride,
Throw doubt, and sail with joy the honied tide.

III.

All things are full of labor. Bear thy load,
    For in the doing thou shalt have delight.
    The pressèd juice of grapes will sweeten, night
With million stars shall light thee on thy road
To Edens. Happiness in thine abode
    Shall wear tiaras golden, and "the light
    Not found on sea or land," effulgent white,
Shall dome above thee, life be one long ode.

So, drink of gladness; chase the yellow bow;
    Find bag of gold; be happy butterfly
And woo the gilded glories round thee; go
    Among the clover, where the grass is high.
And be a lad again; the melody
Of nightingales be one long song to thee.

IV.

The thing that hath been is to be ; then love,
    And flowery brides, and beauty, holiness
    Of heart and soul. So, bring thy bridal dress,
And bring the crushèd rose that heaved above
Thy heart at Hymen's altar ; then a dove
    Of Ararat you seemed to him, not less
    Than eve's one star ; while love with gentle stress,
Pressed life's new hope, and flung the wedding glove.

So, dare remember all the joys that were,
    The bridal wreath, the lover's stolen kiss,
And fall upon thy knees once more to her,
    And try to win the beauty and the bliss
That once were thine when life was fresh and new,
And every rosy sparkled in its dew.

V.

No new thing 'neath the sun? Ah me! Ah me!
    Where all our hopes and aspirations? Say :
    Shall inky night befoul my marriage lay?
Shall every hope and aspiration be
Dethroned, and relegated to the sea
    Where Hope's new wings were clipped? I tell thee, nay !
    Fling out Hope's banner to the light of day,
And sail fore'er with gladsome Jollity !

And build thy gilded castles in the air,
    Raise minaret and turret to the sky,
And on thy tombstone Hope and not Despair ;
    Fling flowerets like a rainbow up on high ;
Be merry as the flowers, make old things new ;
'Twill build a hope from heaven down to you !

VI.

And no remembrance?   Ah! to thee, gray hairs,
    Shall be oblivion in thy hoary age :
    Thou canst no more unclasp the hallowed page
And read : In orchard 'neath the mellowed pears
The rosy god entangled me in snares
        Of love! and there in love's assumèd rage
        I stormed and stamped.   But last in gilded cage
He prisoned me, I captured unawares.

And so he shall not turn these hallowed leaves
        Of memory, shall not dare recall the flowers
Of bridal days, when 'neath the mouldered eaves
        He plucked them, crowning all the happy hours
With life's new wreath, and breathed a tale to her
That made life's viols sound out merrier.

VII.

And I was king.   And so a king am I ;
    I shall not be dethroned.   My gilded rod
    Is bright with age.   I climb with silvered hod
The building that I build.   The hours may fly,
The clouds may gather in the rounded sky,
        And thunders crash above me : flowered sod
        Shall smile in loveliness up to its God ;
For Hope doth bow above us far on high.

So, once a king, be king for aye : let Time
        Roll on in chariot car, and days and years ;
Hold fast thou hast, and life shall rhyme and rhyme
        In one glad song ; and all thy falling tears
Will turn to beaded gems, and every thing
Will grow to beauty like a jeweled spring.

VIII.

And he was preacher.   Let no tale of woe
    Be preached to me.   I'll fling my starry flag
    Against the clouds.   Wilt call it tattered rag?
An emblem of defeat?   Let tidings go :
Happiness still spans like overarching bow,
    And he who dares to say my golden bag
    Is empty, finds my banner does not sag,
But floats o'er every hut and bungalow !

Go ! the Procession moves apace.   The star
    Of hope is on our gilded ensign ; back
We look and forward.   O'er the sanded bar
    Of death we never go.   The beaten track
Of glory, hope, we march with rythmic feet,
And on our banner is no word Defeat !

IX.

I gave my heart to seek all wisdom.   Time
    Flew on.   The days were wedded to the years
    In haloed glory.   Here was death with tears,
And here was love with many a marriage rhyme,
And here was wisdom, genius in his clime
    Of song, and high court-ladies with the peers
    Of Parliament, and some had jibes and jeers :
But, over all, Omnipotence sublime !

I squeeze the orange, and my hope is there,
    I press the grape, and rare delicious wines
Of Magra touch my lips.   With golden hair
    My muse has come ; with corrugated lines,
Like crinkling waters, rippled down her back
Her golden hair, sweet flowerets in her track.

X.

Yea, I have seen all works beneath the sun:
    But dare not tell me vanity, that all
    Is vanity. A builder build a wall
I 've seen, to shelter little children won
From murky streets, and then caparison
    Them all with heaven's happy coronal;
    I 've seen a mother with a remnant shawl
Bend homeward, her last scrap of duty done.

So, lift the glory of this mundane sphere
    Against the stars. We may not raise the dead;
But death has won our heart's unstinted tear;
    And, therefore, shall we cry when she is wed?
Nay, nay, take not our hope! Let cloudless skies
Expand with golden rainbow o'er our eyes.

XI.

Our ways are crooked?   Who shall make them straight?
    But pardon, we will fling our flowers to thee,
    O Heaven! We 'll sail our life's tempestuous sea
With all things fair, and Hope shall be our mate;
Our crew the best! To come here was our fate,
    Yet we dare hope our song will rise and be
    A rhyme among the stars, Eternity
Will hear, and God find waiting at the Gate!

So, let us place a rosy on her grave;
    So, let us mourn when we are sad and drear,,
And let us sing o'er death our solemn stave,
    And drop above our dead the silent tear;
And when we lay her in the quiet tomb,
O let us feel she 's smiling thro' the gloom!

XII.

And never man had greater wisdom : I
    Was ruler; I communed with mine own heart;
    Yet vanity.   O preacher! let mine art
Place love's embroidery o'er the earth and sky,
A veil of beauty over death, with dye
    Cerulean paint all woe, the flowers that start
    O'er new-made graves, transpose to heal the smart
Of dissolution, hallow those that die.

Since I, O Preacher! now would change all woe
    To beauty, and make death a glorious hope :
This life a preparation till we go
    In grand procession thro' the doors that ope
To Heaven; for I have come to preach of love.
And hope, and of that Wreath of flowers above.

XIII.

I gave my heart to know all wisdom. folly :
    And yet I found vexation.   Why this sadness?
    Obliteration of all hope?   This madness
With things that we call beautiful?   O jolly
Hand-maidens, pouting girls, drive melancholy
    Over the caverned Styx ; and boys of gladness
    Blow all your trumps of joy and chase this badness
From earth and twine the Michaelmas green holly.

For I have drawn a flaming sword, and hero
    In life's great vanguard, I shall lead to battle
For peace, and white contrition ; every Nero
    Shall feel my blade ! We 're not "dumb, driven cattle,"
But human gods with spirits born in heaven;
With strength of one?   Yea, as the strength of seven!

XIV.

Yes, in much wisdom there is grief, and so
  Does knowledge cause us sorrow. Yet, dear Bard !
  Inspired by heaven, I love the daisied yard
By cabin home, the lovely flowers that blow ;
I love to see the rainstorm's yellow bow
  Across the mountains, an embroidered card,
  A chiseled cameo, a poet starred
By earth, with banners flaunting high and low.

For hear my mandate, doubter, infidel :
  This life is but a premonition grand
To me, of that high life where faretheewell
  Is never spoken ; where a wingèd band,
Like great white clouds, throng our Jerusalem,
White-robed and crowned by starry anadem.

XV.

And so avaunt ! all doubt. Serene and fair,
  Come sweet Placidity, and happy girls
  With wreathèd horns, and love-entangled curls,
And flowery bosoms, apple cheeks as rare
As Eden peach, with rippling golden hair.
  And winy gladness, tangling gray old earls
  In meshes of delight, revealing pearls
In pursèd mouth, and hearts as light as air.

For melancholy, trials, troubles, all
  And everything that comes to mar our mirth,
Get hence and leer behind thy dungeon wall ;
  For fairies shall adorn our lovely earth,
And dispositions sweet as pressèd wine,
Shall be to all of earth from heaven divine.

XVI.

Go place a rosy on the bride, a ring
    Of gold bring unto her. Make merry. Paint
    All splendors of the morning. Make a saint
Of her. Put on thy wedding suit and bring
New gladness unto her. The bridal spring
    Put in her heart. Discoloration, taint,
    Disfigurement, and woe, and all complaint,
Put these aside, and basket roses fling.

For, hear again : I come to battle worry,
    And disaffection, sour entangled creeds,
And stop this strain for wealth, this hurry, hurry ;
    This mad contention ; trample on the weeds
Of old hallucination ; fling about
The seeds of peace, and crush this age's Doubt !

XVII.

I 'll build me castles by the sanded sea,
    I 'll raise me houses full of all things fair,
    I 'll be a lover of old books so rare
That earth has not another. I will be
As free as soft Balalo gales, and tree,
    And shrub, and vine, and vert, and voweled air
    From thrummèd lute, shall come from everywhere,
And please me with their braided rarity.

For, jolly girls, be jollier still, and swains,
    Pipe out new songs ; and cow-boys fling your hats
Against the clouds, and send the Bacchus strains
    Down into hearts of gloom ; and pastoral mats,
And Turkish rugs, and everything of beauty
Bring to our lives ; for 'tis your right, your duty !

XVIII.

Place rare bouquets upon your shelves ; fetch art
    From every clime, and sculpture-work of Greece.
    And all the love of Dante's Beatrice,
And Ariosto's Princess. Laura. Start
In all directions ; love to shrine the heart
    With all things beautiful ; and find release
    From foul-faced woe. till tessellated Peace
Shall smile eternal, tho' death fling his dart.

And music bring, and viols tunèd rare.
    And lutes that Orphean hands shall touch, and lutes
That blessèd Sapphos loved ; and maids with hair
    Of gold, and marble boys, white little mutes,
And all things fair, till jolly cheeks of joy
Are red with love. life's buoyant as a boy.

XIX.

Burn Voltaire. Never read a bitter book
    Of theologic doubt ; and never gaze
    On prurient picture. Come from out the haze
Of turgid isms, and never dare to look
On horrors. Down, force down the gnome and spook,
    And rush among the fields, the tasseled ways,
    The greening grots, where beauty 's all ablaze,
And life outbabbles like a grottoed brook.

So, turn your shoulder. Drive crowned Satan back.
    And crown alone the god of love and peace ;
Pile high the flowers along life's winding track,
    And crown with all the loveliness of Greece
Your home, your fireside. and thy shrine will be
Lovelier than emeralds of antiquity !

XX.

I said in mine own heart: O go to now !
     For mirth shall prove thee, and sweet pleasure.   And
     He found it vanity.   Take, belov'd, my hand,
And let me lead thee with thy noble brow
To quiet pleasures, rosy mirth; endow
     Thee with sweet love; the Spanish saraband,
     Or stately minuet, or dance on sand
Of seashores, be as pleasures, I avow !

Since I would have the golden lyre, the lute
     That beauty touched, the stringèd harp; for mirth
Is mine.   I'm not a preacher tall and mute,
     But blessèd being God has made for earth,
Its wholesome joys; and love I beauteous spring,
Mine own true heart will crown me like a king !

XXI.

And laughter's mad?   And mirth what doeth it?
     My laughter keeps me sweet; and mirth?   Ah me !
     I give thee gloom, and death, the moaning sea;
But laughter, mirth, I cannot spare a bit;
A thousand bumpers I will drink to wit,
     A thousand beakers drain; and I will be
     By laughing waters, full of joys, and see
An Eden, build me castles where I sit.

For hear me, pessimist, there's not a woe,
     An unremembered grave, but I would clothe
In loveliness!   Let every floweret blow;
     Strike down the weeds of doubt, for these I loathe;
And bury woes in garbs of loveliness,
Yea, clothe them ever with life's wedding dress.

XXII.

I sought to give myself to wine ; I built
   Me houses grand, great works I made, that I
   Might see what should be good for men. And, ay!
He planted vineyards; boys in figured kilt,
And Bacchus lads, wine-bearers ; bossèd hilt
   On rare Damascus blade, and elf and fay,
   And music-boys in many a roundelay,
He might have had, and yet his wine had spilt.

For all the gold of India pilèd high,
   Or eagle diamonds flashing like the stars
In winter skies, had not sufficed. For I
   Know Peace! She 's found beside the milking bars,
And not where temples rear their fronded art,
For these delight the eye, but not the heart!

XXIII.

He made him orchards, gardens : luscious fruit
   O'erweighted many a tree, and bellied grapes
   Blushèd in purple splendor, greening capes
In viny textures spread above ; and mute
Waters soft mirrored treetops ; spiral chute,
   And curvèd strait, and curious-made escapes
   For water, vines in old fantastic shapes,
Made his new kingdom, yet it did not suit!

For nay! He had no wine of gladness. Eye
   And heart were not united. Method, yea!
Method was in his madness. Fie and fie
   For him! He might have livèd to this day
And he had been dear earth's unhappy wight,
A little pleased, but happy? Ah, not quite!

XXIV.

And pools of water he did get, that trees
    And vines and herbage he might have, for life
    To him would be a passing dream.   The strife
Of kingdoms vexed him not; no rarities,
Nor dainties, with their trite disparities
    Or disaffections; but the pruning knife
    Every false tree should feel, till rare and rife
Earth glory he would worship on his knees!

But Love he knew thee not!   And wreathèd Peace,
    Your A. B. C. he never learned; for gold
And glitter, and the glimmering things of Greece
    And Rome, or rare exotics from the wold
Of England blinded him.   Satiety came
To him.   Today we do not know his name!

XXV.

And yet he got him servants; maidens fair
    As angels are he got.   Great cattle, too,
    Nibbled his grasses.   Yearling calves did loo
In o'erabundance.   Any Crœsus there,
Or far, was never richer.   And I swear
    Solomon in all his glory, yea! to you
    I say, was never greater.   Through and through
The land he hunted, seeking all things rare.

Ne'er greater king reigned o'er Jerusalem!
    And yet, O Preacher! crowned with carcanet
Of pearls of price, an envied diadem
    Of glory, where's the beggar you have met
Whose footstep was not lighter? whose leal soul
Had not its own Venitian barcarolle?

XXVI.

He gathered silver, gold: and of the kings
  Around, all treasures that peculiar were
  To such, he gathered.   Nothing did deter
Him; for this man would have all earthy things,
And maids of beauty with their sparkling rings
  Of love; and singers rare, and lutes that stir
  The harmonies within us.   Juniper
In whorls of threes, and knot that flies and sings.

And yet was woe across his fields; his house
  A palace e'en, was not a Paradise;
He envied men; and e'en the little mouse
  Nibbling forbidden meal.   Yet handsome Nice
With whirling dust, or any city far,
Had been to him a brighter rising star.

XXVII.

So I was great.   My God!   And yet he cried:
  Vanity!   O build me pleasure-houses rare
  As Aidenn, and a fabric make me fair
As Barberini Palaces; and dyed
In dyes of gods, new osier baskets: wide
  As love or heaven raise my castle there,
  And make me pontifical, and my prayer:
O this is all for which I sigh, have sighed!

But, happy builder, architect divine,
  Thy structure lacketh in its chiefest part!
It has the arabesque, the curvèd line,
  But O 't is cold.   It lacks a human heart!
And so I turn me to my cottage home,
And love will king me like a king of Rome.

XXVIII.

His heart rejoiced. But list his varied tale
    Of interchanging joys. His eyes desired ; ·
    And craved his heart ; and so to him transpired
A tale worth telling. But, ah me ! a wail,
A rich man's sigh, comes o'er the intervale
    Where tropic roses bloom. He had aspired
    To all things meet. But now he has retired
To arbor nook. But care has made him pale.

And yet how great he was ! All maids of song,
    And instruments attunèd rare, and bards
Of genius, aye ! a multitude, a throng.
    Of rosy-footed joys, and flowers from yards
Of Eden flockèd round ; and yet he said :
All 's vanity ! Better far that I were dead.

XXIX.

And then I looked on all the works my hands
    Had wrought, and all my labors. But, ah me,
    Ah me ! He found no pleasure. O'er the sea
A ragged sailor starteth home. The bands
Of love, a mother's ; and the golden strands
    Of love, a sweetheart's, draw him, make him free
    Of spirit, and he smiles. His bended knee
Is holy as he strikes the shining sands.

And he was poor, but richer than a king,
    And he was rich, but poor as poor could be,
For one alone the whole year long was spring,
    For one the days went tossing like the sea
On rocky shores ; since one had bargained for
His peace, the other's came by natural law.

XXX.

And madness, wisdom, folly. These to him
    Were potent. But O such discouragement
    In all his life. Had he a man's intent
Who loveth love, and God, and genii dim
Are never floating o'er him black and grim
    In midnight's solemn hour, he had not bent
    With gilded woe. And, ah ! he had not lent
His goodliest days to folly's nacent whim.

And yet he saw his life mistake ; so, ay !
    More bitter grew his bitterness : no thing
As wholly new as life could money buy :
    All things had been : in fall and purple spring
He found no newness. Thousand years before
As kingly kings had done his doings o'er.

XXXI.

His dust may be my valid self. But I
    Am speaking from a heart that loveth gold
    That it may clothe the poor, not build me old
High turret castles, that the passer-by
Will halt and worship, as beneath the sky
    It glimmers to the morning. O'er the wold
    I 've seen me catafalques, and bells have tolled
For what? Alas ! for rich man that did die.

Oh give me bags of gold, the wealth of Ind :
    But give me sweet Valhalla maidens, yea !
To scatter my great wealth. For I had sinned
    Against myself, had beggars by the way
Seen useless millions in my strainèd purse,—
But don't misunderstand me in my verse.

XXXII.

O great ecclesiarch, I envy thee
   Thy wisdom! Folly had a reason, nay!
   And darkness; a great governor or Bey
In Turkish lands; the earth; and roaring sea
In its eternal restlessness; the bee
   On wayside flowers; and in the shining way
   Of love, bride-garlands. Preacher, yea and yea.
Thou sawest all, but peace flew far away.

With dirty urchins, one, and two, and four,
   I've seen a beggar king upon this throne
Of love and home, suggestions of that shore
   Where life's eternal, not a tare is sown!
So who will tell me wealth means happiness?
That it will clothe us like a papist's dress?

XXXIII.

And so the earth-fool is as I? We die
   The death of life; but I am wiser far;
   O'er him I am as some resplendent star;
Some shining glory; gemmed tiaras lie
Close at my feet; the pageants passing by
   Are unto me; that gaudy chariot car
   With trumpets blown and songs, sweeps down afar,
For I am king, and likened to Most High!

But no procession passeth for the fool:
   And yet the pageant's soon forgot, the herse
With tasseled horses; in the wayside pool
   Throw veiny pebble; such the rich man's verse!
The rich and poor have each the same earth breath,
But who shall draw the line between their death?

XXXIV.

The high and low are soon forgot, unless
    A touch of heaven does link us unto Him !
    For I, and hear me, tho' the thing be dim,
Dare say in all this age's worldliness.
There is a God ! So don thy spotless dress,
    And dare be brave where armèd Doubt is grim,
    And isms ; for Heaven is no new poet's whim,
But fact ! So, bow the knee, and dare confess.

For look ye in the lives of infidels, _
    And look ye in the lives of those that doubt :
The first is but a life of sad farewells,
    The second, very lamps of life are out ;
But he who hopes beyond the mouldered tomb,
Sees Him of Olivet across the gloom !

XXXV.

And so he hated life ; for vanities
    Upstarted here and there, and grevious were
    His works to him, and like a whippèd cur
He skulked in thought.   The salt unresting seas
Were not more restless.   Wine-cups to the lees
    His lips had quaffed.   Valkyrian, e'en her
    Of Odin, spear-mark made, and like a bur
It harrassed him and took away his ease.

But blame him not, for life had taught him ; say,
    · Was ever wiser ?   Life to him had been
A learnèd lesson.   Had he gone astray
    In doubt, he had not touched the carvèd kin
To holy song ; but God had made him rich
In goods, though Time hath left no marble niche !

XXXVI.

He knew not if a wise man or a fool
    Would reign o'er all his great estates ; and so
    He moaned.   Where lilies turned their whited blow
. To God, he stood with folded arms.   The cool
North breezes touched his cheek.   Sevastopol
    Had less contention.   In a dream of woe
    He stood, but every grass-blade seemed his foe ;
His endless sea had dwindled to a pool.

He caused his heart despair.   His labor vain
    It seemed, and all his goodly acres round
Seemed folly, since he soon must cross the main,
    Be buried in the churchyard's sodden ground ;
I venture tears outglistened in his eye,
With wealth so much, at thought he soon must die.

XXXVII.

His days were sorrow, and his travail grief,
    His heart no rest.   And yet 'twas best to eat
    And drink, be merry.   These to him were sweet
Savor to his sad plight.   But bordered leaf,
And broken stone are trite.   Yet, Time, the thief,
    Has stolen name and fame.   The winds repeat
    The funeral dirge.   In spring or summer's heat,
We guess his early history, for 'tis brief.

A wise man wrote Ecclesiastes.   Stave
    Of requiem had never been so sad ;
Ah ! we hunt vainly for the Preacher's grave ;
    For e'en his gilded name and all he had,
Are perished !   Yet how little do we seem
Before the greatness of this man !   I dream !

XXXVIII.

Yea, dream and dream and dream.   But, ah to me
    Cometh the thought : All things have seasons.   There's
    A time to live, to die.   The ripened pears
Are mellowed to their fall.   Eternity
Is wide as mercy.   Dread adversity,
    And death have seasons.   Climb life's weary stairs,
    And at the top is death.   A time for cares,
And love and wine and glories unto thee.

A time to kill, a time to heal, to weep
    O'er death's intrusion ; time to laugh and mourn,
For life hath levels, and her roads are steep,
    The heart will weary, every soul be torn :
But hope is radiant, above all woe
It spanneth ever like an endless bow.

XXXIX.

A time to get, a time to lose, to weep :
    And yet is life worth living.   Pretty flowers
    Are strewn upon the grave of babes, and bowers
Of fragrance rare are made for them.   Why keep
Such sacred trait?   Because you know the sleep
    That binds their loveliness, will break in hours
    Not far to be, tho' now the black cloud lowers,
And death o'ertakes thy baby ere it creep.

And yet a time to love, and now if ever :
    For never is a holy mother's heart
So sorely touched as when death does dissever
    Her from her newborn babe.   The tear will start,
E'en when the flowers have faded on its grave ;
But God that took him, and 'twas God that gave.

XL.

A time for war, a time for peace. But hear :
    O love thy neighbor as thyself.   Let strife,
    And battled field go by the wall.   The knife
Of internecine bitterness, the spear
Of tasseled knights be buried.   Let the ear
    Hear village hautboy, and the air be rife
    With gladsome music.   Lead the flowery wife
To scenes of loveliness, and glad the year.

Put flowered housings on thy steed, and ride
    To tune of drum and fife ; but let thy battle
Be for sweet peace.   The tally-ho with bride
    Head the procession.   Let no musket rattle
On hostile field, and crown with olive leaf
The whole broad land, and place a rose on grief.

XLI.

Hear : Everything is beautiful in its   .
    Own season.   Firstlings of the flock, the herd
    In meditative days.   Let lucent word
Go forth for hope.   For time so softly flits
Across our lives in its new parceled bits,
    It seems the flitting of a robin-bird,
    A zephyr that a faded leaf has stirred
In winter nooks.   But go where beauty sits.

For beauty is the queen of every land ;
    Love all things fair ; love not the sombre weeds
Of mourning.   Wipe the tear, and with the hand
    Of kindliness, and to the tune of reeds,
Lead in all loveliness, and all things fair,
And veil with flowerets every home's despair.

XLII.

I saw the place of judgment. Ah! 't is well :
  The good man's judged already. Only fear
  Is to the wicked. Be ye of good cheer,
And smooth the wrinkles from thy face. I tell
Thee He is coming! Let no infidel
  Dethrone thy hope; for even he on mere
  Of death, will look to God with falling tear,
And Jesus' name be in his last farewell.

Judge men by deeds, and not by bandied word ;
  Let sense prevail, and he that takes thy hope,
Forget his name. Go seek the singing bird
  In pastures new ; climb up the flowery slope
That leads to heaven, and dare be true and brave,
E'en at the open mouth of thy child's grave.

XLIII.

The beast and I the same earth breath? And yet
  I dare be more, dare imitate the One
  Who made the stars, the slave, the Scythian Hun
Who conquered old Pannonia ; who set
The rainbow in the sky ; who 'll not forget
  The sparrow in its fall ; who sent his Son
  To die for us. Dare do as He hath done.
And rise o'er beasts like towering minaret.

For e'en tho' death should be the end, 'tis better
  To rise with glory like a star, and shine
With splendor. Dare to break the rusting fetter
  That binds our lives to doubt. Oh be divine,
And when the last great hour shall come to thee,
Thy earth-reward be hope, not vanity !

XLIV.

Yea, all will turn to dust. But of the pure
    Are lilies made. But dust to dust ! Be wise
    As serpents ; 't is the spirit on emprise
Of valor, rising like an incense sure
Of God ! White Galatea on earthy tour
    Thro' moulder's mind, before a thousand eyes,
    Was lifeless in her clay. Snap not the ties
That bind. Be wary of the Fauns that lure.

Fling hope and love to every home ; let joy
    Dance nimbly, timbrel sound, and fiddle play,
And morris-dances come, and maiden coy,
    And crimson sky, join in with roundelay,
Till every heart is full of gladness, hours
Go by like fairy's dream among the bowers.

XLV.

Yea, better is an handful with a heart
    Of quietness, than both hands full, with woe,
    And discontent ; so make amends with foe
And enemy, unselfish be in art
That comes of wealth. Give each poor beggar part,
    And sleep shall come to thee ; since as ye sow,
    So shall ye reap ; and such a sleep, I know,
Will come to thee as babe's in crowded mart.

For peace and sleep and happiness are more
    Than gold, than hoarded wealth ; for riches oft
Annoy the night. Stand on the rocky shore
    Of ocean, beacon banner hold aloft
To threated ship, and such a peace to thee
As gold has not this side eternity.

XLVI.

Go 'mong thine orange groves, thy vineyards rare :
　　Pick purple clusters, fling them to the boy
　　With knee-frayed pants; and set life's rosy joy
A-dancing.　Pluck the mellow, yellow pear
For gift to rosy maid with golden hair
　　In wavy ripples; to Jack Tar: Ahoy !
　　Come feast, Jack Tar !　Forget the old bell-buoy,
And breakers, and our pristine homage share.

For giving makes a man.　And he is king
　　Who 's king of self.　This life is but a span :
If some to spare, outdo the blooming spring
　　In glad abundance.　Laurel old King Pan,
And make him play a rural ditty sweet
As love, and all the zephyrs will repeat.

XLVII.

Put spangles in her hair ; twine chains of gold
　　Around her neck, embroider every doubt
　　With starry loveliness ; throw each hand out
With gladsome fullness ; dance across the wold
Among the daisies ; let all stories told
　　By sweet new dabsters all along life's route,
　　Be told again ; and kiss away the pout
Of beauty, and joys will be manifold.

I 'm here to laugh and not to cry.　The tear,
　　Ah me ! let teardrops come from happiness :
Have hope.　Don't make this life a funeral bier,
　　But clothe thyself with joy and loveliness ;
And fill the whole great world with gladsome song,
And shower with flowers the world's great surging throng.

XLVIII.

I 'm sick of sadness.   Tell me of delights
   In shady nooks, and take me bosky ways
   Of dewy freshness, where the lightsome fays
Dance on the green in cloudless starry nights.
With merry lads and lassies, pursy wights
   In life's gray prime, where song and voweled lays
   Sweeten and harmonize the soul; for days
Are flitting fast.   So, come !   Enjoy the sights.

Make gardens : bury up the earth in flowers
   Of beauty, garlands make as nattily
Arranged as bridy dreams ; and laurel hours,
   And minutes, seconds, and as prettily
As ever flowery bride : for hear me now,
I 'd place a crown on every being's brow.

XLIX.

For once you lose desire ; ah me, ah me !
   The grasshopper shall be a burden, things
   That once were thy delight, will take the wings
Of morning; and thy friends will be to thee
As naught; for now thou thinkest of the Sea
   'Twixt Him and thee; and other summers, springs,
   Are nothing now !   Now nothing pleasure brings,
But, sans desire, from earth you 'd gladly flee.

For now like throneless patriarch of Rome.
   Your mind is busy with the future state.
Because thou goest soon to thy long Home,
   And dear old memories cannot make you wait :
For earth is fading like a bitter dream,
But e'en thro' death thou seest the great throne gleam !

L.

The son of David, he hath said these things
    Of beauty, wisdom, to another time,
    Now faded out like some old poet's rhyme
That echoed with a great heart's questionings
Of busier life and death, when other springs
    And winters hoar, in far and elder clime,
    Were pregnant with the great God music-chime
That only the divinest poet sings.

And yet today a new world scans the pages
    Of gray old life, to gather from their lore
And spoils of years, the mystery of the ages
    That only on that far unknowable Shore
Is sure revealed.   And yet we may not grope,
For, at the end of every life is Hope!

LI.

To some this life is full of vanities;
    To others rainbows span from shore to shore;
    And one may mourn his love, his lost Lenore:
And one may fill his life with charities;
And two may wed and find Idalian Dees;
    And one may walk alone and bravely soar
    Across the mountains; others may adore
The Being smiling over sapphire seas.

But, high or low, no theologic doubt,
    When grimy death draws near, can take our hope;—
For, hear: 'Tis hard to put our God-lamp out,
    E'en though in bitter darkness we may grope;
Since over all our life's great weal and woe
Ever, forever spanneth heaven's bright bow!

LII.

And so the Preacher may not have a grave,
    No mausoleum of Carrara stone;
    And yet the ages heard his great voice tone,
Tho' poet sing his sad funereal stave
As over one who lived.   So, do not rave;
    For though he sleepeth in white death alone,
    Nor any note of lyre or voicèd phone,
Still let the pleasant grasses o'er him wave.

His golden words are ours.   But vanity
    Shall fade away like some distorted dream
Of Hades, and across his widening sea
    We still shall sail to him, the bright white gleam
Upon our sails, reflect the loveliness
Of his great life that came from God to bless.

LIII.

One generation passes; graves are wide
    And yawning.   Yet, and yet the bridegroom comes
    Arrayed with beauty.   Birds still peck the crumbs,
And like a rainbow cometh life's new bride,
And with a rosy in the eventide
    A little ditty or a carol hums.
    And Cupid does his hymeneal sums.
And smiles between them when the knot is tied.

So, generations go, but others come;
    And these will pass like panoramic dream;
And yet the earth remains.   The busy hum
    Of life is in the valley.   Yet the stream
Of death is ever winding to the grave;
But even there, let's sing our life's best stave!

LIV.

For singing makes the glory of the sky
    Even more glorious, gives a rare new song
    To busy earth, and glads the passing throng
With reminiscent ecstasy ; for I
Would add a tint, a hue, a trancing dye
    To every field, and touch the golden gong
    To lyric melody, the fiddle plong
And pling, as life's procession passeth by.

So, come fair nymphs, and maids of Plato love,
    And lads and lassies full of music rare ;
Descend ye glowing Nine, while stars above
    Twinkle in beauty, and the cooling air
From southern climes, soft woos our willing cheek
Till we are pure as stone-entrancèd Greek.

LV.

The sun will rise, and yet he will go down
    And leave a glory on the western hills,
    A pure white loveliness upon the rills,
And in a farewell twilight to the town,
Slow fade in beauty. Not a passing frown,
    But wreathed in smiles : for over woes and ills
    I 'd spread a texture lovely, wove in mills
Of gods, and coronaled by flowery crown.

For I would add a color to the bow
    That spans the storm, a hue to lilies white
In odorous valleys : and with Cupid go
    To music-lands, and 'neath the German night,
Lit up by stars, cry out : "Another song !
Fill up the glad red beaker to the throng !"

LVI.

The wind may sail away to southern vales
    Of sweet deliciousness, and not return ;
    But I will place a rosy on her urn,
And let a teardrop fall where Zephyr wails
Among her funeral lilies, say : "Sweet gales,
    Enwaft my love to her, and with the hern
    From Scottish Dees, and all her beauty turn
Angelic, breathe upon my placid sails."

For winds may go, and death may come, but I
    Shall grasp the promise of the clouds ; the tear,
Ah me, that comes unbidden, and the sigh
    Shall pass away : for faint and far, but clear,
There shines a halo with a hope to me
That spans across the great Eternity !

LVII.

The streams may surge and join the great blue sea ;
    My ships with bellied sails may blow away ;
    . My soaring lark may vanish with his lay,
And yet my heart-song still remains to me ;
For though the earth pass on, eternity
    Remains ; and though I own the earth today,
    'Tis nothing if the bright and starry Way
Is hid, I cannot say : "I go to Thee !"

For though I paint me splendors in my halls,
    And build me arches groinèd to the clouds,
In marble basins have me waterfalls,
    I cannot hide from thee the clinging shrouds,
But walk a living Superstition vast,
Until the disembodied soul has passed !

LVIII.

No man may utter all the thoughts that lie
    Hidden within his being; and the ear
    Is still unsatisfied; and year on year
Goes unrewarded till his heart and eye
Give up the quest, and earth and moonless sky
    Pass onward unrecorded; yet as clear
    As clarion morn or lusty chanticleer,
The Morn of morns shines out to you and I.

But, will we learn? Ah me! the golden god
    We build, and shining monuments upraise
Against the stars; the pontificial rod
    We kiss, and strut a king of passing days;
And yet a tinsel potentate, ah me!
Of earth, but not the great Eternity.

LIX.

My song is but a repetition; I
    May strike the lyre, the voweled notes are dim
    In unremembered ages; raise to Him
A pæon of triumphal praise; the sky
In vaulted glory in that other by
    And by re-echoed it; a spectre grim
    Arises from the past with every whim
And trick, that last resolve to you and I.

And yet is repetition sweet to me;
    For thus I win my rosy back again,
My ox-eye daisy down across the lea;
    And spring will come and summer too, and when
Old Winter comes to every soft retreat,
I know that spring her beauties will repeat.

LX.

But, is it new?   A Whitman grand and gray,
    The good gray bard of Camden-side, essayed
    A metre new in language great arrayed ;
And so the world has lost a Poet's lay
That might have echoed to the farthest day ;
    For great Miltonic thoughts were there displayed,
    With Emersonian grandeur.   Muses prayed :
"O take us through the old accustomed way !"

But nay and nay, with language of a god,
    A meaning vast as Avon's tragic bard,
The sceptre in his hand, Apollo's rod,
    The good gray poet is uncrowned, unstarred !
And yet his numbers were a battle-ode ;—
He was too vast for such an earth abode !

LXI.

There's no remembrance !   In the elder times
    Now unremembered, did the great God reign
    In glory? was there such a Cuba? Spain?
A British empire? undiscovered climes?
The master verse? the bardling's halting rhymes?
    Did hostile falchions glitter on the plain?
    Were ever such disasters as the Maine?—
Upon our newest fad the ivy climbs !

And yet I would remember other days ;
    The old associations, bygone hours ;
The old familiar faces, and the ways
    Our fathers knew ; go backward to the bowers
Where dewy love first told his new old tale,
And birds sang love to every intervale.

LXII.

Yea, over Israel he was a king !
    But who can point his place of sepulchre ?
    Ah ! was it Solomon ?   I dare demur :
Koheleth ! rise and end this questioning :
But through the winter and the passing spring
    The silence is unbroken.   Juniper,
    Anemone, or e'en the bitter myrrh,
May know his grave, or birds that fly and sing !

"Yea, I was king o'er Israel !"   O son
    Of David ?—But the voice is hushed for aye ;
And yet, *Koheleth*, were you Solomon ?
    The god of wisdom in that elder day ?
But Grotius denies it : wherefore we
To bandy or impeach his sovereignty ?

LXIII.

And though he sought all wisdom in the earth,
    And in the great dividing sea, in lands
    Beyond the sea, and where the golden sands
Exposed their granulations, where the birth
Of kings took place, and men of drink and mirth
    Made merry nights, and gray old Morris bands
    Danced light fandangos on the babbling strands,
He moaned his fate ; for in his life was dearth.

And yet the great One reigning far, unseen,
    The Ruler of the earth, he ever held
In highest estimation, more than queen
    Or reigning king ; and from the lore of eld
Brought magic splendors to enhance this One,
The Father who would give his only son.

LXIV.

Yet, Septuagint! his name we dare dispute
    With lore of ages. Was he Persian? Where,
    Where did he reign? And was he David's heir
Apparent to the throne? All tongues are mute;
No language such strange figures can compute;
    And so the Maccabees may sway; for there
    By Hartmann he is placed: and yet I dare
Name him the man the very heavens can suit.

For out of all his toil and moil and woe,
    He rises like a star, and points on high,
The realm of peace, where Hope's o'erarching bow
    Resplendent shines across the great wide sky,
And tells us if we penetrate the night,
Behind it all the great sun shineth bright!

LXV.

Accept the crooked things of life, and be
    A happy ministrant to every ail:
    Go pick the flowers beside the babbling vale;
Send out your ships upon the restless sea;
Plant shrub and vine and flower and cedar tree
    On all thy slopes, and in the intervale
    Place mirrored lake, and on it silver sail,
And romp with nature in her rarity!

For purity and nature's rare delights
    Oft come of suffering; so weal and woe,
And bitter days, make pictures in the nights
    With Titian moonbeams, and the gamboling doe
And swift gazelle; for hearts that are not tried
A many a lovely blessing is denied.

LXVI.

Let knowledge, love and wisdom come to thee :
    Let fine appreciation grace thy mind;
    Find beauty in the meadow, and the wind
That plays a ditty in old nooks; agree
With nature; hold thy natal liberty
    For aye, and love the earth and be resigned
    To life, to all; and once you are refined
As gold, your life will babble like a Dee.

For songs within the heart can never die :
    And e'en when death has come to thee and thine,
The old songs will re-echo like a Wye
    On English meads, and coarser ones refine :
The Cotter's Night in Burns's canty rhymes,
Still echoes with the ingle's merry chimes.

LXVII.

Wisdom and grief go hand in hand.   We look
    On frescoed walls where art has reigned.   We see
    The palace ships in freighted majesty ;
We stand in wonder by some pearly brook ;
We read old nature like an open book ;
    In awe we stand beside the great wide sea :
    A crannied flower has piqued us; far and free
The winds have come from some deserted nook.

A blade of grass has dashed our wisdom down ;
    A twittering bird has held our learning up ;
We cannot cross our rural, native town,
    But mysteries shine within the daisy's cup ;
So, wisdom gives a certain kind of grief ;
I am dumfounded at a mouldered leaf !

LXVIII.

But I will prove with mirth this world of ours,
    With shining star and hornèd moon; with bird
    And flower, the lambkins and the pasture herd
Feeding upon the slopes. So, Bacchus, towers
Of grapes to thee; come, Ida, to our bowers,
    And we will sing the wine-song Bacchus stirred
    To revelry, the juicy-tippèd word,
With purple grapes distilling winy showers.

Since mirth is mine; I 'll be a happy wight,
    Tho' tasseled horses draw my lady's hearse;
For even then the stars will splash the night,
    Since death has won an angel. Sweet and terse:
"And death has ta'en her to the highest star!
But death has ta'en her where the angels are!"

LXIX.

And laughter, what of it? 'T is savor rare
    Of aching gout; it is a poppy pill
    To drowse you sweetly in a Lethe rill;
It drives the man of saddle-bags. So fair,
So pouting sweet and softly debonair
    It makes the rosy maid; you pause to fill
    Your life's best being, feast upon her still,
Yea, feast upon her face, her sparkling hair.

So, court the god of laughter; woo the maid
    Who smiles the whole year round; be good to her;
For she 's a sylph in ecstasy arrayed;
    The lovely nightingale may sing and whir;
The lark of morn may soar afar; but she?
She 's Queen of everlasting Jollity!

LXX.

And did I say I 'd give myself to wine?
    And say I 'd pull the purple clusters down
    From mossy nook?   That I would hide my frown
In flushes of the grape?   That wine 's divine!
That it can beautify a friend of mine.
    And make him finer than he is?   Renown,
    Imagined kingdoms it can make; can drown
The bitter soul, send boating on the Tyne.

So, pull the purple clusters!   Drink not deep,
    But just enough, my pard, to sweeten thee;
And just enough, perchance, to make thee leap
    With joy.   But, nay!   The breakers of the sea
Are in the red wine cup!   So, have a care.
The red, red wine may turn thee to despair!

LXXI.

I builded houses; I 'd the wherewithal
    To make a name on earth, a money-king;
    A prince of princedoms; gods should touch the string
On harp of gold; and archèd room and hall
Should echo music, till a drowsing thrall
    With murmured meanings, birds with sparkling wing
    In slumberous tune, should soft and drowsily cling
To pictured nook, to pictures on the wall.

But, ah! is tinsel beauty such to him?
    Can money buy the dearest peace he craves?
I see a spectre disembodied, dim!
    I see a sexton!   Is he digging graves?
Alas, alas, can wine and money buy
God's kingdom?   No!   For I am ever I!

LXXII.

O make ye orchards; raise the lucious fruit;
  Put borders on thy gardens; train the vine
  On mossy arbor; make old earth divine;
Place marble Cupids by a winding chute
Linèd with flowers, and statues sculptured mute
    As new first love, uprear in tasty line,
    So poet eye, enraptured by the Nine,
May find it Eden, rare and lush and cute.

And yet is happiness within the heart:
    You cannot win the bulbul's gladsome song
In barrèd cage; you bury dross in art
    Of Raphaels, yet this you is you!   The throng
Can read your heart in every line!   Bright gold
Can never cover sores or wrinkles old!

LXXIII.

With artificial pools, the haunts of fish
    Of varied hue, you may enhance your place
    Of earthly habitation; yet your face,
The index of your mind, will show the wish
Unfound; thy goodly friends will come;—but, psh!
    The vintner, where his vinelets interlace
    In lowly cottage, goes a better pace.
And has contentment in his savory dish.

So, spread your acres; build your turrets high;
    Make deer-parks; have a dainty hound or so;
Make Michael splendors that shall glad the eye:
    But still remember woe to you is woe,
That though the purple cover with its art,
It cannot hide the moanings of the heart!

LXXIV.

Your servants may abound ; your herds may line
    The everlasting hills ; your heart may swell
    With natal pride, and life's new Christmas bell
May ring out gladsomely, and to the eyne
May come the love of flowers ; the curvèd sign
    On marble bust of thee, (like rose in dell,)
    May add a sweetness, though a faretheewell
Be in the odor, end in spillèd wine !

But, hoarded Wealth, has Peace enshrined thy form
    In happy wreathlets ? Has thine ardent friend
Arrayed thee like the bow across the storm
    In Springtime ? Do the colors softly blend
In unadornèd art ? O let me lead
To thatchèd cottage bordering on the mead !

LXXV.

And you may gather silver, yellow gold
    From hidden mines : the stringèd harps may play
    Old classic poems ; night may shine like day
In Oriental pallor ; citterns old
In unforgotten songs, in tune unfold
    Their music, flower-boys wreathèd, join the lay,
    Till many-voicèd maids, with cutest sway,
Come hying from the wood or English wold.

But, trainèd songsters, can you pipe a song
    To hearts of gloom ? Can great magician's spell
Of rapt enchantment veil a single wrong
    With fine delusion ? Come across the dell :
Her dress is scant ; but look down in her heart :
Her song is sweet, but innocent of art !

LXXVI.

You may be great to outward eye; the brook
    May babble in your fields; the sparkling trout
    May shimmer in your pools; the sloping route,
The winding path may lead to osier nook
O'er tillèd field.   And yet I read your book
    Of bordered gold; but you have blotted out
    Reality!   Cute gold-gods mime and pout;
Yet you are you; you cannot hide that look!

So, women, wine and tunèd lute can not
    Disguise your self; for when my lady fades,
And wine-cups cloy, and softest lute has caught
    Your, melancholy, little shining blades
Of retribution pierce your callous heart;
For you are you yet, under all your art!

LXXVII.

Your heart may dandle every joy.   But, come
    With me, a little runlet crosses here;
    And there, a natural lake is sparkling clear;
Beside the lilacs, where the bees may hum,
A rustic grotto smiles; with savory gum
    Spruces are standing; lusty chanticleer
    Pipes out his clarion to the budding year,
With bordering vine and tree and rustic plum.

And in the midst a cottage.   You and I
    Would give our wealth for such a simple home
Were peace included.   But, ah me! we sigh
    Because we live in France instead of Rome;
Because our money will not buy us peace;—
But moss is on the monuments of Greece!

LXXVIII.

But, is there profit in the chase for gold?
    The race is to the swift. A hundred years
    Will raze us to the dust. Alas! our tears
Of life! what mean they? With our arms we fold
A lovely child. A few short years and mould
    Is on her tomb. From every shadow peers
    A writhing face, and many a teardrop blears
The page of life; and more when hearts are sold!

So, fling your wealth in golden showers; lead love
    And joy and peace across your threshold; take
A sip of nectar; stars will shine above;
    Throw out your ducats for the children's sake;
Divide your gold with love; for it will be
A bridge of flowers to Eternity!

LXXIX.

So I was great. Ah! great in what? In lands?
    In cattle? sheep? I see a mother, she
    To me is great in ideality!
He tunes his instruments; and noisy bands,
With fifers, stamping feet and clapping hands,
    Are honoring his great glory. But to me
    A higher glory is that sovereignty
That crowns a mother in her life's new sands!

But greatness is a thing of taste, a whim
    That Fashion names. For one is crowned by Love,
And one by Gold, and one by only Him
    Who moves the clouds. I see a star above;
And is it some old dear departed guest
Who dying said: "Thy will be done, thou blest!"

LXXX.

And he indulged in every joy ; in art
    With curvèd line ; in architecture grand
    As time had seen ; in kine and fertile land ;
In prancing stallions. Yet how fared his heart?
His curios from every foreign mart ;
    His porcelains from distant shores, from strand
    Unknown, were beautiful ; but hand in hand
Two lads are happier with a broken cart !

And yet was God an essence pure and fine
    Amid his lavishments ; and tho' he cried :
    "Vanity !" he felt the great One was divine,
    And Him of Nazareth they crucified ;
And yet his pleasure-houses grew apace,
And were the rare embodiments of grace.

LXXXI.

One sings his Annie Laurie, and is king ;
    One pipes a ditty on an oaten reed
    Beneath the stars ; another mounts his steed
And rushes on to fame. I cannot sing,
And yet I'm happy with a fiddler's string
    And bow. Some pluck the daisies in the mead ;
    Some sit beneath the slanting sun and read
The glories of the rainbow in the spring.

For one hath pleasure in an ambling pad ;
    And one takes pleasure in a boat at sea ;
Another still is happier when he's sad,
    And melancholy days are on the lea ;
For Autumn odors are like scented breath
To him. He loveth to commune with Death !

LXXXII.

So, who shall say that I cannot be I?
    And who shall say that you shall not be you?
    One loves the rose; but I the mournful yew;
Some sail with gas to find an arctic sky;
And one is ruined by a sparkling eye;
    One loves the rose that's beaded in the dew;
    Another loves it faded!   Skies are blue;
And yet our puzzled life is "Why?" and "Why?"

We never reach the goal we set.   We soar
    Above the clouds.   'Twas but a freak of will:
We are brave Nelsons when the breakers roar
    Against the adamantine rock.   The rill
Has made a river going to the sea;
But you are you, and we are simply we!

LXXXIII.

But I will build a bridge of flowers to God;
    For earth shall pass away.   I pay the toll
    To death, and die.   But shall I lose my soul
For fleeting earth?   I love the goldenrod;
I love the flower that decks the mouldering sod:
    I love to see Ambition reach his goal;
    I'm sad when Sidney Laniers hearses roll.
And all my being crieth: "Maud, Maud, Maud!"

So, here the gist: "O build for heaven and earth;
    O build thee mansions for the glowing skies
Of Immortality; make second birth
    As pure as vestal love; sith he who dies
A child of earth and heaven withal, may be
A king of kingdoms in Eternity!"

LXXXIV.

So, win this world, and dare be true and brave,
   Even when martial music rends the air,
   And people with a wild theatric stare
Lose sanity. Earth is but a monstrous Grave!
Ah me! our proudest flag may float and wave;
   But Bonapartes are thrown. We climb our stair
   With tinkling steps. And yet how oft Despair
Is at the goal, and sings our funeral stave!

And yet I'd grasp the very stars; for life
   Is larger to the curbless soul. He serves
Who only stands and waits! But, in the strife
   I'd mingle. Genius is a mass of nerves
In Poes! O me! to be without desire;—
May Orphean hands retouch the broken lyre!

LXXXV.

His hand has lost its cunning. Dumb and dead
   The great harp lies. No more the master touch
   Shall call the melody; yet his art was such
The heavenly harmonies he seemed to wed
In such a married cadence Orpheus shed
   A glory on his head. He wooèd much
   In youth and prime. But now his nerveless touch
Is vain; for all his art had vanishèd!

And yet he sang his swan-song: "O'er the Bar!"
   When Death was knocking at his being's door;
He seemed to rise in glory like a star;
   The Muses took his pen. "Nay, nevermore!"
And England's magic singer passed away;
His ashes honor England's great Abbàye!

LXXXVI.

But why palaver?   Who can make a grain
    Of mustard?   Yet we Ingersolls have dared
    To weigh the Universe!   I had despaired
Myself these years, had not a certain strain
Of finite reason, told me o'er the main
    A Paradise is waiting!   I'd not cared
    To live this life of earth had my mind shared
A Voltaire's doubt!   For with it life is vain.

But people grasp at earth.   Long in the night
    The candle burns, and man goes speeding on
To what?   An earthly phantom of delight
    That fadeth with the purple of the dawn;
At death he'd have a pocket in his shroud!—
To die like us he is almost too proud.

LXXXVII.

Leave city walls and hie to rural vales;
    Leave business cares and come across to me;
    The city is a dull satiety;
But come and jump with me the old moss rails;
Let's gad like boys thro' dusky intervales;
    For here is Nature clothed in rarity;
    And here is Nature's amplest liberty;
The wildbirds chorus with a thousand gales.

And then you'll think of God!   For He alone
    Hath made the beechwood flower, the gadding vine
In beauty's tangled nooks, and on the stone
    Placed mossy loveliness, while lavish wine
From far ambrosial lands outsparkles red
Where thousand vines have over-canopied.

LXXXVIII.

And these are Intimations of the Land
    Beyond the stars; since everywhere is God;
    In meadow vale and waving goldenrod;
In woods, and old fence flowers on every hand;
The beechen tree with wildly woven strand,
    Outdoing art in naturalness. The sod
    With its commingled loveliness, where nod
The wildflowers, by the Southern zephyrs fanned.

And so my song is full of Intimations
    Of Heaven, such as every heart may see
In vale and valley, in the rare creations
    Of God! And let me say in song to thee:
"Win earth, and all thy heart may rightly crave;
But win that other Life beyond the grave!"

LXXXIX.

How beautiful is Lycidas in song!
    How beautiful are flowers upon the walls
    Of crumbling abbeys! What fresh coronals
Has Nature placed upon the grave of wrong!
Upon the grave of Pompeys once so strong
    In glittering Imperialism! But calls
    The blackbird by a Cæsar's ruined halls,
And o'er their dust still tramps the Roman throng!

For Cæsars only won the crown of earth;
    They only wade thro' slaughter to a throne;
The widow with her mite may win the birth
    That crowns with everlasting life alone;
For did she not give more than all the Jews?
But he's not best who sits in costliest pews.

XC.

In In Memoriam what beauty shines!
    In Adonais how the thought expands
    In beauty!   Lycidas in Milton hands
Is rival; and the English laureate's lines
Still crowd them hard.   For these are Malmsey wines
    Of song to me.   The grapes of many lands
    Have made their nectarine.   Love's golden strands
Have bound them.   See him hidden in the vines!

And so the glory of the sky is here
    In love's untrammeled song.   For Muses nine
Caught splendors from the heavens above the mere;
    Put rhythmic numbers in the poet's line,
Till such the beauty in their pictured art
We tender love's best offerings of the heart.

XCI.

Wisdom excelleth folly.   Be ye wise
    In preconceivèd work, and fleeting Time
    Will give thee lore from Oriental clime
Where pearls may glitter to enraptured eyes;
Where God's great sun in happy, vaulted skies,
    Smiles graciously.   And hear the onward chime
    Of never-ceasing worlds.   And yet the rhyme
Of His new Paradise still hear, since lies

Heaven forever at the end of life!
    For though ye win the shekels of the gods,
And go about this world in purple, strife,
    Contention, war, shall rage about thee;   sods
With Love's heroic blood shall still be red;
But win the bay that crowns the Christian dead!

XCII.

The Queen of England!   Here is earthly glory;
- The Tsar of Russia!   Here is earth renown;
    Our President may wear Imperial crown
And still lose Heaven!   Our Gladstone old and hoary
Is crowned by Love!   But Corsicans are gory
    In butchered blood!   And hostile cannon drown
    The cry of Pity!   Some are great in town;
A Stevenson is great in trancèd story!

And yet I'd call ye from this vain Ambition
    To that great Moment when the highest King
Must bow!   For Love, and Life, and white Contrition,
    Are more than these!   Yet, love the purple Spring;
The vagrant Summer.   But in loving them
Lose not that never-fading Diadem!

XCIII.

Go under cooling stars, and walk amid
    The quiet glooms, and solitary be;
    For I would have you touch Eternity
Alone!   Go seek the mouldering graveyard hid
In tangled briar; not where doughty Cid
    Lies buried in his pomp, but where the tree
    And amorous vine, in wild serenity,
Have made the only earthly pyramid!

The tangled brushes cross the path; and here
    Are Death and old Neglect!   There's not a friend
To place a flower, no eye to drop the tear
    Of sympathy!   But who can tell the end!
For once was beauty nurtured here, the eye
Of Pity mutely turning to the sky!

XCIV. ·

The mouldering stones make only trite appeal
    To our humanity; and Memory
    Has lost the chain, once Love and Purity
Welded with golden links. The zephyrs steal
In crooning lullabies; but can you feel
    The touch of love? Some died in Chastity!
    But who were they? And did they cross the Sea
Of jasper? Only Heaven can reveal!

But pause amid this Desolation. Here,
    Mayhap, a king is buried, or an earl
Who wore the ermine. Who will shed a tear
    Above their dust? Red amethyst and pearl,
Or nectar of the gods can never save;
Find Heaven, and conquer mystery of the Grave!

XCV.

But read ye, if ye may, the fate of these;
    They joined the grand Procession to the Grave!
    A hundred years, and like an ocean wave
They vanish ever, and forever! Seas
Now roll between. But fall upon thy knees,
    And while the waters of Oblivion lave
    The shores of Memory, sing a quiet stave
To Death; for here he has his sovereignties!

And while ye kneel, O ask the willing Heart:
    "Is Earth or Heaven my Principality?"
I do not curse thee, for I love thine art;
    I love the real, great Reality
Of life. Yet earth shall crumple like scroll!
But, will you win it and lose your own soul?

XCVI.

I love to hear the harp in quiet days;
    I love to hear the birds in jargonings
    Of song; the crows in guttural caws in Spring's
New life; I love to hear the blackbird's lays
Among the wakening hills; I love the ways
    Of happy childhood; and the whirring wings
    Of migratory birds a memory brings
To me of ever-vanished yesterdays!

And yet I dream my dreams, and visions chase
    Each other through the channels of delight
That lead to Him! For there I see His face
    A shining glory! Far across the night
My vision is a vision unto me
Where reigns the Nazarene of Galilee!

XCVII.

I love the earth; how beautiful to me
    No muse can tell; I love the babbling brook
    That stealeth to the sea; I love to look
At emerald breakers dashing from the sea
In organ cannonade with majesty;
    I climb the hills, and like an open book
    I read the page of Nature. On his crook
A shepherd leans in rapt tranquillity.

And these are pictures that have chained my heart
    To earth! And sometimes comes the thought to me:
"How can this Heaven be lovelier?" For art
    And Nature, masterly and curiously,
Have made our earth so beautiful, I say:
"Can Paradise be fairer in that Day?"

XCVIII.

But, draw the bow, and be a citizen
   Of wholesome pleasure; dare to win the love
   Of minstrel maid.   And yet the stars above
Are looking on thee.   Be a denizen
Of Faery.   Yet, beyond your mortal ken
   A star is shining; and a spotless dove
   Is winging.   Toss the gem and tinsel glove;
Pour out the ink, and lay aside the pen!

For, lackaday, the world has won your heart!
   Ye cannot serve two masters!   So, have done
With acting!   Worship 'gen the sculptor's art:
   The fashioned jewel, and the diamond won
From kingdoms in the earth, and drink the wine
Of Bacchus, putting off the One divine!

XCIX.

And yet these holy Intimations are
   The true outpourings of a human heart;
   I would not clothe them in adornèd art:
But ere you cross this life's great Harbor Bar,
O find that fadeless, everlasting Star
   That shines in Heaven!   And then the wingèd Dart
   Will lose its sting!   Since in the crowded mart
E'en Death will come, and Life's funereal car!

For, such is life.   But life is bounded by
   Death!   Heaven alone will never pass away;
So, win this world; but win across the sky
   That other World; and when the Judgment Day
Shall come, a crown of glory shall be thine,
Beautiful and fadeless from a Hand divine!

C.

Turn down the glass that held the sparkling wine
    Of pristine days; eschew the ballet now,
    And take the wine-crown from thy wrinkled brow;
For these are days that you should be divine
In heart; for you are marked by facial line
    Of cards and dice, by cares that make you bow
    In gloomy attitude.   The great Ship's prow
Is nearing its last port across the brine!

So, let the glad days be a memory gone
    In faded mists.   Forget the glittering bar
With portly tender, and sail surely on
    To that great Haven beyond the western star;
For now the glory of the earth is past!
'Tis Heaven or Hell you have to face at last!

CI.

The moon has smiled upon thy face; the skies
    Have arched their welken over thee; the stars
    Have shone upon thee with translucent bars
Of light; but soon a mist will cross thine eyes
Forever!   To his home the eagle flies
    On buoyant wing; and e'en the pasture bars
    Are just at home!   But you that conquered Mars
Are homeless!   Out of reach thy heaven lies!

So, close the game; throw down the loaded dice;
    A knock is on thy door at last; for Death
Is no respecter!   Rules of coarse or nice
    He knoweth not.   A pestilential breath,
And weeds and lovely flowers together lie:—
In losing Life the very soul shall die!

CII.

Once Love and you went hand in hand, and all
  The skies were flushed with Hope's new radiant smile;
  You sailed for aye to some Hesperian isle
Of song and fruit. No interposing wall
Of Eden harrassed. Earth thy banquet-hall
  Of flower and jest and wine. With snare and wile
  Only sweet Eros came in prankèd style
Of new delights, with many a winding mall.

But all has changed. The light has faded out;
  The earth seems like a ball of rolling mist;
At last you've ta'en the never-swerving route
  Of life. But Love and you have met and kist
The last lip-kiss. And yet I'd hold out hope;
For e'en at death the Gates of Pearl are ope!

CIII.

You may be sitting at your humble meal;
  You may be dining with a king in state
  With glittering crown of gold; but Fate, e'en Fate,
Will dog thy steps. The rosy red may steal
Across the pallor of thy cheeks; the peal
  Of tinkling glasses half and half translate
  The music of thy love: yet added rate
And rate, thy coming doom will half reveal.

So, when the Angel comes to thee with scroll
  Of faded years, e'en then forget thy gold,
Thy loves, and from the ruins save thy soul;
  Since now desire has gone; thou art too old
To care for petty gewgaws of the earth;
Now Heaven is beauteous as a flower at birth.

CIV.

And yet one glimpse, one faint Auroral flush
　　Of Life, is all the hoping heart requires
　　To toil along to death; for such desires
Are heralds of delight; and fruits are lush
And ripe, and life's new rosy's modest blush
　　Is on the cheek, and bands of voicèd choirs
　.　Sing seraph songs, and all along the wires
Come song-tones like sweet bells in even's hush.

And yet a throw of chance; for one transgression
　　Leadeth across the Styx.　Thy cap and bells
May be a safeguard; for the fool's confession
　　Is surely: "Crown sometimes a doom foretells!"
Temptation is to those of finer mould;
Beauty is sought, and beauty can be sold!

CV.

He plays life's ditty on a mellow flute;
　　One plays it with a cymbal and a gong:
　　A Burns has sung it in a Highland song;
Another in an attitude as mute
As statues dreams it.　Down a little chute
　　A brook is scampering to a busier throng
　　In cities far, perhaps to some Hong Kong;
But who another's song would substitute?

For you would still be you, and I e'en I;
　　My song may be from out a simple heart;
And you may love in cedar shades to lie;
　　Another still love art for only art;
But what your song, no matter, high or low,
Some aimless fingers o'er the strings may go.

CVI.

The clock will strike; but let it strike at last
    The final stroke.   Why should we care for this?
    We turn our lips to win the farewell kiss
Of love.   Perhaps a kindly hand will cast
A spray of lilac on our casket.   "Hast
    Thou loved us?"   In the Aidenn vales of bliss
    The question may re-echo.   Things amiss
May then be righted when our graves are grassed.

And yet we lay the old coat by; the boot
    Is wrinkled, and the clothes are frayed; and we
Are worn and running down; but let them hoot
    Their owl-notes to the moon, a jasper sea
Has snowy barque awaiting at the dock,
And heaven is ours no matter what o'clock.

CVII.

I do not know?   Go pull the briar and rose;
    Go win the sailing lily on the stream;
    And take thy little meed of salt and dream
Thy nights away, for these are God.   Night knows
Her crowned white queen; and every flower that blows
    On wayside fells.   But ope the magic Ream
    Of Life.   Thy name is writ thereon!   The gleam
Of Paradise is where the west sun goes.

For you have won the radiance of the stars
    Of white Eternity!   And though the clock
Strike three or one, to you the silver bars
    Are shining.   You have heard the final knock;
And crowned for that Valhalla of the skies
Thy death is sleep to thine immortal eyes.

CVIII.

At old Uxmal palatial ruins lie
    In glorious crown of weeds and gadding vines;
    And yet a perished hand hath made these lines
Of ancient days; at Teocalli high
The mouldering stones are piled.   The song, the sigh
    Of winds are here.   The red Lepanto, wines
    Have drowsed their memory.   And the lichen signs
Of old Decay are on them, far or nigh.

The work of man shall perish from the earth;
    And yet he buildeth better than he knows
Who builds a temple for that higher Birth
    Beyond the sun and stars; and orange bows
Shall span above him; and amrita tree
Shall bloom for him beyond mortality!

CIX.

This higher criticism; ah!   What of it?
    Is God the object of their search?   Is He
    The object solely?   On a chartless sea
I fear they sail.   What one can spare a bit,
A shred of His great book?   Come, go and sit
    At Jesus' feet!   And let the Bible be;
    The more you tamper, more the Deity
Will disappear; the dove of hope may flit.

'Tis well enough.   We cannot spare the whale,
    Nor Jonah; they are sacred to the Book!
Take these, as soon destroy the rended Veil,
    Saint Luke, or John, or James; since as you look
In these, a hundred things may meet the gaze
That puzzle you.   God's ways are not our ways.

CX.

Accept the rose ; who put the fragrance there?
  And see that wildflower by the winding wall :
   Who placed it there? that ivy crowning all
In dainty amorousness? Her cheek is fair
As fragrant flowers, a wreath of golden hair
  Vaileth her face. Are not these wonders? Saul
  Did miracles. Moss and ivy cover hall
And palace. Wonders meet us everywhere.

A blade of grass has mysteries for me ;
  An apple-blossom typifies a thought
To some. The great commotion of the sea
  O'erwhelms my heart, and therefore I am not
The one to take a single word away
From that great Book of books! 'Tis nay, and nay !

CXI.

We often build to beauty with our thought
  Aerial habitations of delight;
   We place our statues in them marble white,
Till everything to beauty has been wrought ;
The pillared roof, the walls with silver bought
  In foreign lands ; the stars that gem the night
  Have lent their lustre, till a happy wight
We sit, for all our fancy has been caught.

So, build these happy fabrics of the brain ;
  Dream dreams and have thy visions of the night ;
Be herald of a merry-footed train
  Of joys ; but, never let it leave the sight
That all this loveliness will sometime fade,
And that the last earth-tune may soon be played.

CXII.

One loves his German coat of arms for aye ;
    Another Russian ; and Italian blood
    Would flow for Italy ; and in the mud
The hostile foe would trail our Flag. The lay
Of Highland clans would sound in Scottish fray
    With pibroch notes. The roses red may bud
    And bloom on all alike. Some Captain Dudd
May show his stars ; but I am I that Day !

So, empty honors, what are they ? We strut
    With titles and a golden uniform ;
But wipe away the battle's grime and smut ;
    Forget the tattered flag, the leaden storm
Of strife ; will any gloried shoulder star
Be passport sure at that eternal Bar?

CXIII.

In archæology of Jewish lands,
    Egyptian or Arcadian, the bard
    May delve ; the scholar here is crownèd, starred ;
Antiquities are but the golden sands
Of Yukon vales to him ; his velvet hands
    Are soiled by mould ; he 'd give his dearest pard
    To delve in spoils in some Assyrian yard
Of old, where not a mausoleum stands.

But these are earthly loves, the intimations
    Of sure obliteration and old Death :
For all the martial, pantomimic nations
    Of earth have marched with unabated breath
To that eternal silence of the Grave,
Where only life's defeated banners wave.

CXIV.

Great aqueducts in Roman lands may flow
    With waters of the gods; but best of these,
    Is great Campagna round old Rome; are trees
Amid its ruined glories? Once the bow
Of happy skies o'erarchèd here. I know
    Of Asia, Spain and Greece and France, but glees
    Of wildbirds echo in their ruins. Lees,
With mournful waves, sing glories long ago.

So, touch Divinity, and span the years
    Of Time; for Rome and Greece shall pass away
Forever! Statues with their marble tears
    May stand in classic shades; but when that Day
Of days shall come, the monuments will go,
The Sphinx and tomb with not a line to show.

CXV.

My Preacher telleth there is nothing new
    Under the sun; so Rome was Rome before,
    And Paris Paris. On the New World's shore—
New? African or Pole or wandering Jew
Were here great æons gone? Beneath the blue
    I walk; the little auk may rise and soar
    Above me. Nay. Extinct. And Nevermore!
Is writ on Iceland, Denmark where he flew.

We build Love's dearest monument to last;
    But soon the ivy finds its chiselèd base,
And moss obliterates the name. The blast
    Has blacked it. Few short decades and no trace
Remains. But he is building better far
Who builds his monument beyond that Star!

CXVI.

But, sing a new song; don't be gloomy, I
    Would touch the riftless flute; for love and songs
    And bridal marches, happy-footed throngs
Of minstrel maids and boys, a starry sky,
With endless bright processions passing by
    In gala dress, with cymbals, golden gongs
    Of melody, are not classed among life's wrongs,
But are life's blessings ere the body die.

The hand that arched the rainbow o'er the storm
    Has filled our cornucopia with flowers
Of every hue; and we may deck our form
    With fabrics of the loom, and crown the hours
With rosy-footed joys. Yet, more than this;
A time will come to take the last earth kiss!

CXVII.

Place ampyx on thy hair, a fillet band
    Of loveliness, a snood of tasty art,
    A diadem, a crown; but keep thy heart
Unsullied. Rings are pretty on the hand,
And in the hair an evergreen or strand
    Of laurel. Go in beauty to the mart,
    And ride in nice coupé or fangled cart,
But ever have in view that cloudless land.

Long-faced Religion, 't is the creed of men;
    For my religion laughs the whole day long,
Sith Paradise is ever in the ken,
    And every heart-pulse leapeth in a song;
Nay, nay, religion is to sweeten me,
And sweeter make my sour humanity.

CXVIII.

Pour out the ampul oil ; these sacred things
    Are beautiful in pure chrismation, I
    Feel holier with the holier vessels nigh ;
I love to hear the church-bell when it rings
Its Sunday matins, or in vespers sings
    Religiously.   The stillness of the sky
    Seems stiller, and as music floateth by
Dies off in half religious questionings.

The firebells and the wedding bells may sound
    In variant note ; but great cathedral bell
Gives us uncertain sound ; and in a swound
    Of His religious glory dieth.   Spell.
With images of cherubim, hath held
Us thralled, as memories from forgotten eld.

CXIX.

The Indo-Chinese architecture, grand
    In half fantastic-like imaginings ;
    The temple of Confucius with its wings
Of sculpture, great Pagoda, make this land
Unique ; for here the sculptor's cunning hand
    Hath wrought with inspiration.   Yet there clings
    A reverence false, kaleidoscope of things,
As purposeless as pictures on the sand.

And yet hath beauty reveled in this clime :
    Some phases in a certain line of art
Teach that a subtle cunning and a rhyme
    Of trainèd workmanship in many a part
Of Indra's temple, or Madura's fine,
Hath made the whole or kindred parts divine.

CXX.

Spread dust upon the tablets; trace for me
    A diagram of loveliness, and paint
    Ideal splendors, tracery as faint
.As soft Auroral flush, and like a sea
Of glass, repose in beauty, with the tree,
    Or vine, or Tuscan abacus; a saint
    At vespers, with a holy plea or plaint
To that white One of ideality.

And give me Grecian Doric, with the trick
    Of chiseled workmanship, Corinthian,
Or Roman Doric; yet the candle's wick
    Is burning to its ebb. A Caliban
May win our true life's everlasting goal.
Worship this loveliness, but save thy soul.

CXXI.

With low abasèd wing bow not thy head,
    But bear thy chevron like a god, thy shield
    Of dented glory on contested field
.Of valor: let no battle's sun set red
O'er thy defeat, though mountains of the dead
    Appal thee. What thy battle, never yield
    If Right be on thy banner. And dare wield
The axe till every hostile foe has fled.

And yet there is a braver fight for thee;
    Yet not a host with banners floating high
Above a thousand spears, but Purity!
    The quiet hue of unimpassioned eye;
The half unconscious glory of a soul
That leans on God with murmured barcarolle.

CXXII.

Put on thy red abolla ; I have naught
    To wager 'gainst the glory of the land
    Of song and love ; and I would head a band
Of cloaked centurians ; for every spot
Of earth is glorified to me. I fought
    The battle of the soul. My works shall stand
    Imperishable, though the crumbling sand
Be scattered, if the keystone breaketh not.

I love the glory of the soldier ; I
    Admire the banners of the rank and file ;
I love to see Old Glory in the sky,
    The burgee float o'er some historic pile
Of Britain. Envy hath no place for me,
But perfect Freedom's universality.

CXXIII.

Put deft acanthus on thy pillars ; build
    A thousand glories for thy palace ; rose
    And intersecting vine commingle ; bows
Of knotted flowers in stone have workman skilled
Place beautifully, as some divinity willed
    In realms of loveliness, and in repose
    Soothing to love ; for dainty tracing goes
To beautify, and life's glad heart is filled.

I 'd love to be this king in marble home ;
    I 'd love to sit amid these statues white ;
And just as daylight meets the darker gloam
    Of starry eve, and whited queen of night
Saileth in sea of clouds. And yet to me
That other Mansion shines more gloriously.

CXXIV.

Yea, have your brave aceldama on slope
   Of Hinnom, so it please thee; but the vale
   Of Eden booteth more. A boat with sail
Far out to sea, may hold thine earthly hope,
And through the sea-night darkness you may grope
   With only love that dares the starless gale
   Of heaven; and this is better far than wail
On Jewish Hinnom, earth thy horoscope.

But minds are different; one adores the muse
   On starred Parnassus; one aceldama
To bury strangers 'neath the mournful yews
   Of some Jehoshaphat; a falling star
Draweth another. But the intimations
Of Him are in minutest earth creations.

CXXV.

Yet build your happy Adens in the land;
   Make earth as beautiful as night when stars
   Are dreaming in the blue; make little bars
Of song; go where the breakers roar, and stand
A crowned Adonis; make upon the sand
   The pictures of delight, and hum tra las
   Across the breakers. Now aloft, Jack Tars.
And now alow, to rollers on the strand.

Ye cannot be too happy; drink the wine
   Of new deliciousness, and brim the glass
With juicy splendors of the tipsy vine
   Of love's imagination; gem the lass
With opal clusters. But, O happy wight.
The Bride awaiteth in her spotless white!

CXXVI.

Let winged Vanessa flit from room to room ;
    Let happy-throated songsters sing in cage ;
    Find gem-like splendors on the classic page
Of genius ; have the rarest flowers in bloom,
And put electric stars amid the gloom
    Of shortened days ; with music's note assuage
    . The dissonance of thought, and sweeten age
With gladness as it walketh to the tomb.

Grow flowers to scatter all along life's way ;
    Build Paradises in the mind and heart ;
Play madrigals to dancing sprite and fay ;
    Touch up thy habitation with the art
Of Vinci, make this earth Valhalla fair ;
And yet a brighter one is waiting There !

CXXVII.

Let Juno's Æolus play his harp to thee
    In evening hours ; this earth is sad at best ;
    Since you may have a home, a quiet rest
Of love ; and soon a jar comes in thy glee :
A tear or two, and far across the sea
    Of death, a barque is sailing to the west
    With one so dear ! In white robes she was drest :—
'Tis o'er ; the waves are lapping on the lee.

And yet I'd have you love the fairest child
    Of God ; but if He taketh one away,
Be patient. Hath He ta'en one undefiled?
    Yea, be it so ; and better than astray
In love's defilement. Doth he chasten you?—
Sometimes the heart is softened 'neath the yew !

CXXVIII.

But, have thy ship ahull ; the storms may rise,
    The breakers dash against thee, and the roar
    Of angry waters terrify, the shore
Look horridly beautiful to frighted eyes
As into silver cream with emerald dyes
    They dash in glory. When the storm is o'er .
    The bow, and great ship-clouds no longer pour
Their rains, but sail away to other skies.

And so thy heart-ship, keep her e'er ahull ;
    And so thy life-ship, keep her helm aright,
So when the sun is sinking leaden, dull,
    And clouds in grand procession cross the light
Of Sol, and Storm-King lowers, O thou wilt know
Thy ship is safe, and soon will shine the bow.

CXXIX.

And put thy winglet ailettes on, and be
    A knight of earnèd valor, couch thy lance
    Of trièd steel, and Edward first the chance
Of battle seek, the banner of the free
Hold high in glory ! Dare to cross a sea
    Of blood for honor ! Let thy charger prance
    In barded 'ray, and though a battle dance
Of steeds, let valor crown the revelry !

The fight is to the hardy and the brave ; .
    The glory, honor, to the soldier true,
And ever make thy country's banner wave,
    But, be a soldier in thy gray or blue ;
And yet a braver battle shall be fought
Within the heart, with no escutcheon blot.

CXXX.

Put on thy hanging alb, thy surplice white
  As snow, and dare be brave as Charlemagne
  Crossing the Alps; or wandering, homeless Payne
In vagrant journeyings; hide not thy light
Within the bushel, let it shine as night
  Of summer skies, when not a cloud doth stain
  The starry vault, with Luna in her reign
Of cloudless glory, palely pure and bright.

And then the world will be a fairy land
  To thee, and weed and bush and blooming flower
Will take an added beauty, as the hand
  Of Flora, with an untranslated power,
Had added loveliness to loveliness
Before, and tricked them in a fairer dress.

CXXXI.

For I can see a hint of God in all
  This loveliness; and every sonnet built
  In linkèd rhymes, like gems upon the hilt
Of famed Excalibur, are flowers on wall
Of Eden unto me. A bird may call
  On briery knoll, an ox-eye daisy tilt
  On old worm fence, a drop of dew be spilt
From blooming rose, divinity's here withal.

A hint, suggestion, intimation slight
  As color on the lily, or the first
New flush on summer's rose, if read aright,
  May satisfy the heart; the soul may burst
Th' invisible bonds that bind, and ope the door
To Heaven, far, far across that silent Shore!

CXXXII.

So, find a revelation in the weeds
    By cow-path, or along the dusty way
    Where hurried foot has gone; for night and day
Have revelations unto him who heeds
These things. In crimson-tippèd flower he reads
    Life's mysteries; e'en the dashing of the spray
    Against the pilèd shells, hath word to say
To intimation, nuns with rosary beads.

For Nature is a self-translated book
    To those who care to read ; and Milton read
With sealèd eye, and Wordsworth with the look
    Of wisdom, till the primrose flower or dead
Burns taught him life's acute philosophy,
The light that never was on land or sea.

CXXXIII.

Yea, mount thy white Alborak steed and fly
    To Paradise, to happy Adens far
    Beyond the rising, never-setting star
Of glory. Yet our earth with spangled sky,
And glittering star, a woven banner high
    Above us, is a great round rolling car
    Of grandeur unto me ; and yet the Bar
Of Death is 'twixt us where the heavens lie.

And so as Death is here our latest guest
    On earth, O why not seek that other clime
Where Death is not? For Edens of the blest
    Are ever and forever like a rhyme
Of worlds, the music making music more
And more, as master organs of that Shore.

CXXXIV.

And though thy alca wings be short for flight
    Across the ether pure, refinèd, still
    Unfurl them on the Pyrenean hill
Of light, and sail across the stars of night,
Beyond the crescent moon ; for Death, cold white,
    Is king of kingdoms here; so, wingèd quill
    And pen of gold be laid aside, for rill
Of death is sounding e'er for lord or knight.

And yet the glory of this fleeting earth
    Of destined years is lovelier to me
Than wedding dreams; it hath a music, mirth,
    A symphony of syllabled minstrelsy,
A Beethoven Sonata full of grand
Memorial numbers from a master hand.

CXXXV.

And yet be Queen Alcestis in thy heart
    Of hearts, and some Euripides of verse
    May give thee immortality.   The herse
With empty walls, (where death has sped his dart,)
May rumble darkly to thy curb; 'tis part
    Of life; and so I'd have thee frame no curse:
    But be Alcestis in the universe
Of things, and smile at death's insidious smart.

For there's a glory of the stars, the sun
    That gilds the hills with beauty, and the moon
Hanging like shield of silver, and the dun
    Meadows of Autumn, and the cannie Doon
In Burnsland far; for I would have you win
E'en earth, yet have the angels for thy kin.

CXXXVI.

Get Aldine books of beauty ; vases rare
  As Vestal maids, and pictures where the art
  Is perfect art ; read poems to the heart
From masters dead or living ; bury Care
In flowers ; and grow the peach and mellow pear
  In sunlit orchards ; fetch from foreign mart
  The golden jewel ; let the teardrop start
In love, and thou shalt never know Despair !

For vases, curios and bric-a-brac,
  Adornments of embellished gold, fine scenes
Of sunset lands, all lead along the track
  To Heaven. So, dance across the May-pole greens
Of life : for Eden homes are intimations
To me of Life's ideal associations.

CXXXVII.

For beautiful associations are
  Akin to things divine ; so beautify
  The mind, and go where quiet waters lie
Like silver mirrors ; leap the sanded bar
To bowered isle, and dream a flowery car
  Is bearing thee, beneath the placid sky,
  To some Hesperides, and heart and eye
Will be united, pure as astral star.

And then will mind and soul according well
  Make music on the gold-strings of the heart ;
And life will lure thee like a Christabel
  In half retirement ; sith sweet love and art,
And beauties from a thousand varied climes,
Make Easter music with no jarring chimes.

CXXXVIII.

Be brave as Algebar; the Holy Grail
　　Will come to thee if thou wilt never faint
　　Beside the way.　Have heart and dare to paint
Ideal pictures.　Dare to cross the Vale
Of Tears, and dare put on thy linkèd mail
　　And face the foe.　I love a nun, a saint
　　Of Christ at vespers, but deplore the taint
That kills the fruit, the groan and wryèd wail.

So, be a hero.　Life's a battle-ground
　　To fight the battles of the days that fill
Our years; and never faint at martial sound,
　　The roll of drum, but storm the Lookout Hill,
The high redoubt, the battled palisade;
And yet this panorama all will fade!

CXXXIX.

But though a Washington in glory's cause;
　　And though a Wellington at Waterloo,
　　An Anton Seidl's fate may come to you
In Wagner's funeral march of death; so pause
And think on death to be; for all his laws
　　Are rigid and unchanging.　Dare be true
　　To self, and when thy star sets in the blue
Bright sky, crowned Love will say: "A god he was!"

For Cæsar felt the flush of life, and Grant
　　And Hannibal, and mighty Corsican;
But waves rolled o'er them like a mad Nahant.
　　And Death the victor, stormed the barbacan
Of life, and earthly fame was gulfed in death.
For life to high or low is but a breath!

CXL.

The stately minuet in Pleasure's halls;
    The light fandango with the castanet
    In Moorish lands; the dance on fine parquette
With Gipsy sylph; our land's Inaugural balls,
May lure the heart; the prompter's noisy calls;
    The grand orchestral notes; the lips still wet
    With dance-wine dew; and yet, O Dancer! yet
Music hath fled from Tara's mouldered walls.

For music of the earth will cease at last;
    The whirling waltz, the giddy dance, will end;
But when the fiddle stops, the tone has passed
    Into an utter silence, will it blend
With Death's processional music to the tomb,
When loveliest parterres no longer bloom?

CXLI.

Your gold may build an earthly abatis
    With forkèd pickets, scarp and parapet,
    And you may pay to earth the goodly debt
Of earthiness; and yet the farewell kiss
Of Vestal love, when life has lost its bliss,
    Its song, would be as sweet as castanet
    In hand of Spanish love-maid, when regret
Is all remains to crown a life amiss.

So, crumple up life's luring manuscript,
    And lay aside the gauds and tinsel dress
Of worldliness; for dancing maids have tript
    To earthly measures; and their last caress
Will leave the sting of long-abusèd wine,
Specious and lovely as a Geraldine!

CXLII.

Have dainty candelabra in thy rooms
    Of pleasure ; have thy branchèd chandelier
    Alight, and have Etruscan vase as clear
As still Utopian streams, exotic blooms
And odorous flowers ; have little quiet glooms
    For half concealèd nudeness, pictures dear
    To vanished days, an artificial mere,
And on it fairy ships with shining booms.

And have thy harps and changing æthrioscope,
    And all the handiwork of chiseled art
From far Italian clime ; have carvèd Hope,
    Euterpe, Queen of lyric verse, and heart
And soul will have their highest earthly wish !—
Is satisfaction in this dainty dish ?

CXLIII.

And yet I'd have a world of art for thee.
    The song-bird, mock-bird, and the bobolink,
    The bullfinch, and a little whirling rink
Of treasures ; busts of captains dead at sea,
And Termini of old antiquity,
    And philosophic Hermes ; dainty pink
    And rose, festooning chains with golden link
And swivel, every kind of fruit and tree.

And little silver turnstiles, golden crowned ;
    And noiseless gates of filigree ; in sooth !
The cravings of the heart in Coma swound
    Of earth deliciousness.   And yet that booth
Of hewèd boards, so oft a laugh at Art,
Has held the best effusions of the heart !

CXLIV.

A Portland vase is just as dear to me;
  Mosaic work and parquetry, the nave
  In pillared church, the Anton Seidl stave
Of Wagner song, and orientally
Exhumèd statuary, melody
  Of trancèd Mozarts; and the cypress grave
  I'd beautify, the streets of earth I'd pave
With hope and joy and love eternally.

For earth can be a paradise, a place
  Of peace and song and glory, and a land
Of pure delight. So, turn thy wrinkled face
  Away from lust, be leader of a band
Of happy mortals destined for the skies
Of blinding beauty to our human eyes.

CXLV.

Have not the Shelleys beautified our life
  In song and art? The Tennysons have made
  A witching music in the soul, arrayed
In more than earthly glory. Battled strife
Disarmed by melody! So, sheathe the knife
  Of slaughter, make no red embattled raid,
  But woo all music, for the leaf will fade,
The flower, and death will crown the happiest wife.

For in the grand ovations of this world
  Of fleeting loveliness, all things will perish;
No matter how your banner is unfurled,
  No matter how the fondest heart may cherish
The things of earth, and so my song to thee   .
Is: Win this world and Immortality!

CXLVI.

Wear Venus' cestus to awaken love
    And joy in thousand hearts; have marble boys,
    And Caryates fair; and mixed alloys
Of shining beauty; have a silvery dove
In wingèd marble, spangled stars above,
    A little artificial sky, and joys
    In alabaster, fabricated toys,
And silver boats that dainty·hands may shove.

Have chiseled obelisk or corbel niche
    With fine ogee or moulding rare, a nook
Of builded marbles, tapestries so rich
    In Oriental handiwork, a book
Of poems hath no fine allurements. Yet
How vain, how vain, when dying eyes are wet!

CXLVII.

Have clustered columns, carvèd balustrade,
    The wave-like cyma, dainty fret and foils,
    The feathery foliations, vines in coils
And quirks of beauty, and a masquerade
Of undisguisèd loves, no pasquinade
    Of low lampoonry, not a word that soils;
    Sith here are knights who only use the foils
Of Peace! And yet this fabric fair will fade!

And yet I'd pile the wealth of Ind for thee,
    The treasures of a thousand shores, this earth
Would make as beautiful as love, a sea
    Of never-ending glory; yet, in mirth,
In worldly splendors have one thought for Him,
For all thy proud mirage will soon be dim!

CXLVIII.

I have no word against a happy life;
    I have no word against a happy home;
    I'd have another Golden Age of Rome
For thee; I'd have the banishment of strife,
The quick dethronement of all war; the knife
    Of Spaniard I would sheathe; the golden Tome
    Translate for every country where the gloam
Is thickest, when the hostile word is rife.

I'd crown McKinley with the Wreath of Peace;
    I'd crown the world, the Regent Queen of Spain;
My Country with the glory that was Greece,
    If Love shall reign! Above the mangled slain
I'd drop the tear of Pity; for this world
Is Love. No hostile banner be unfurled!

CXLIX.

So, build thy castles in the air, but think
    On Death! Have pleasure-houses if you will,
    But, listen for that Voice so small and still;
Have pastures green, the lily, rose and pink;
But, weld for aye life's breaking, broken link;
    And build thy mansion on a lordly hill;
    But night and day there is a quiet rill
Running, and soon 'twill reach the final Brink!

So, in these Intimations find the route
    Of glory; dare inherit beauties here
On earth; but never let the lamp go out
    That lights the way beyond the shedded tear;
For life at best is but a passing dream
Of Faery, thousands lost upon the Stream!

CL.

But now farewell, a poet's last adieu;
    A happy singer's last, his parting word:
    His song was not the song of nesting bird
In quiet nooks, but trumpet sounds to you!
And never bard more honest trumpet blew
    Unto his clan!   For with this age I'm stirred
    To might, since these are doubtings I have heard:
"I doubt my Bible and old things and new!"

But I: "Have faith, for life is full of good:
    Large-hearted men and noble women live;
I like to go where Beecher Stowes have stood!
    I know a million silent hands will give;
I know that though a darkness pall the night,
Behind it all the great sun shineth bright!"

THE LADY OF SANTA ROSA

THE LADY OF SANTA ROSA

DRAMATIS PERSONÆ

ANSO, *High Priest of Saturn.*
DON MIGUEL, *cousin of Inez.*
LOLA MORENO, *a Gitano dancing girl.*
DOLORES DE CASTRO, *a Spanish beauty.*
PRINCE HENRIQUE, *son of a foreign duke.*
SENORITA INEZ, *Don Miguel's cousin.*
ALBERTI, *Lola's gipsy lover.*
MIDDLE, *a street clown.*

ACT I.

SCENE I.

Place, SPAIN. *In a room of* FATHER ANSO.
Enter DON MIGUEL.

Don Mig. A goodly morning to you, Father Anso.
Anso. It is a goodly morning, Miguel.
But mornings are not new to hoary Spain;
Since long, long years ago, ere Spaniard lived,
Or goodly Spain was in the almanac
Of time, did mornings blush upon the earth,
The hoary hills, the mountains vast and grand;
And e'en when swarthy Moors held martial sway,
And with their valor dared to conquer kingdoms.

Don Mig. Thy language is as ancient as the hills
Of Spanish empires; thine ideas are gray
As time himself. But ever did old men
Return to buried past, to times agone
Adown the centuries, and so far away
That younger men like me are lost in whirl
Of multitudinous years. But, holy father,
Pray tell me what thou fashionest with ardor
And undenied desire. Since all thy face,
Thy manner, doth betray thine adoration.

Anso. Young man, thou art as splendid as the sun;
Thou art as brilliant as the gloried sky;
And in thy courtly dress of hat and feathers,
And buckled breeches, broidered, flowing waist,
With flowered shoe, and tinseled, silk-like stockings,
And worked by lady's dainty hand, thy sword
With diamonds decked, and filigree-like handle.
Thou art, believe me, Don, the greatest knight
And courtier in all Spain. Men envy thee.

Don Mig. I did not come to woo thy flattery;
For such as I need not the lying tongue
Of Spain's society. I'm as independent
As greatest lord of Cadiz or Peru,
Or any count of Mediterranean waters
That babble out their old salt song. 'Tis I,
O Priest of Saturn, and no other lord;
So, tell me of thy workmanship, this thing
That thou dost fashion to such comely shape.

Anso. By all the powers of heaven and lower earth,
I mark thee for a god of trouble. Beauty
Like thine, and courtliness, and prowess rare,

Will lead to old temptation, which hath sat
On life's high parapet and watched for prey
In coming babe; for loveliness in maid;
For glory, comeliness in thoughtless man;
For gloried fame in some Homeric hero;
A soldier of a fortune high as captains;—
And thus thy dazzling presence will outshine
Thine earthly rivals, till Don Miguel
Becometh star of finest magnitude.

    Don Mig. And thereby falleth from his firmament.

    Anso. Unless thou hast an old man's fortitude,
And such a self-restraint as only gray
Hairs have.

    Don Mig. Then will I paint my hair as white
As hoary snows of winters; for if wisdom,
And fortitude, and self-restraint, and glory
Are the constituent parts of white-haired age,
Then, Father Anso, I, Don Miguel
De Santa Rosa de Granada, will
Grow old so fast my hair becometh white
In single night.

    Anso.   He maketh light of me!

    Don Mig. I beg thy priestly pardon; I must have
My courtly pun. But, hearken, Priest of Saturn,
There's not a man in Cadiz, ay! Nor Spain,
Who beareth greater love for thee; since thou
Art wise beyond thy times. Thou art a prophet,
A seer. And were I in a troublous state
Of mind, to thee I'd hie.

    Anso.   Then thou art troubled?
Old love, forever new, hath late beset thee,

And, like a cobra, still retains his hold.

  Don Mig. Then thou hast heard of this Don's love?
    I see !
All Spain will soon reiterate the story.
But, hark, my Father Anso, I have come
To visit thee with such a tale of love
That e'en the stars do weep. So, lend thine ear.

  Anso. I will. Tho' new this love to thee, 'tis old
To earth as life. 'Tis old to me. But, speak ;
For love hath wingèd feet and tongue, and sleeps
Not till his enemies and friends alike
Do hear his tale of worldly lamentation.

  Don Mig. Thou talkest as old love had late de-
    throned thee.
But, listen to my tale ; for such my love
No man e'er knew or felt a sweeter. I
Lie down at night on grassy mead, and there
Beneath the whited stars, I see my love ;
In draperied room, in festooned bed, I dream
Of beauty's things, the loveliness of ladies'
Eyes. Lying half asleep in semblance strange
Of death, I paint with Raphael beauty, love,
Love, love, with such a train of rare delights,
And pleasures, joys and dainty ecstasies,
That, Father Anso, I would die the death
Of love, if 'twould not break two loving hearts.

  Anso. Thy love is new as newly kennèd star?
  Don Mig. And brighter far than sweet Andromeda.
  Anso. And sorely it doth trouble thee?
  Don Mig.   Yea, father ;
And now I come to thee for solace rare ;
Since, go I 'mong my kinder friends, they smile ;

And 'mong unkindlier, their lips do curl;
So, unto thee I turn as one who will
Judge me precisely, at my finest worth.

    Anso. Then sit thee by me, as by stroke of hand,
And soothing word, to thy responsive eye
I'd lend the glory of mine age, and paint
The picture of thy love-led life. Now speak.

    Don Mig. Her name hath music, voweled too and round,
Dolores ! Was there ever such a name?
'Tis sweet as nectar in old bottles found,
With such aroma unto me, that life
Goes double in its sweetness. Love I sleep,
And love I dream. 'Tis all my life's new business.

    Anso. And never busier man than thou, Granada;
For love will give a wink of sleep when poppy
Leaves, drunk in wine, do hide the petty thought;
Since just so long as thought remaineth stable,
Is paramount, so long will love delay
The hour of sleep. But bards have sung Dolores.

    Don Mig. For such her beauty, such her ravishment.

    Anso. But is she not in everybody's mouth?

    Don Mig. Aye, beggar, lord and count and courtly
        knight!

    Anso. Then jealousy may yet beset thy heart,
Since every courtly clown doth homage pay.

    Don Mig. But I'm a better, since with welded sword
I'll hurl them all to native dust, and she
Will hold me high in favor as the hero
Of many battles.

    Anso.   Once the glory gone,
The cute enravishment that clothes a name
In lustrous beauty, and Don Miguel

Becometh tame, a man without his art;
A duteous husband with a rusting sword,
His epaulets displaced and shoulder-star.

    Don Mig. Then unto newer battles will I turn;
Call forth all doughty heroes of the brand,
And say: I offer unto thee Dolores
As beauteous prize; and any swordsman dare
To face Granada, hath her hand in fee,
If hap so shape his fortune!

    Anso.   Said e'en well.
Don Miguel. But, hearken. What I build
With rarest divination, as you asked me,
Is blessèd heart of Santa Rosa. Such
An amulet as sons of old Poseidon
Dared worship in their lowly holiness.
'Twas at this time, Don Miguel, long gone,
Long years ago. The Trident then was used
By sons of old Poseidon as the symbol
Of fair Atlante.

    Don Mig. Yet from what was 't made?

    Anso. 'Twas fashioned from a great fire opal, which
Was purchased at old Atlan of the west,
An amulet as beautiful as life;
As pure as holy heaven's whitest star.
And valuable beyond imagination!
I prize it as the apple of mine eye,
And, too, as dearest daughter of my heart;
And touched on holy week, it giveth peace,
Tranquillity and hope, enlightenment
Spiritual.

    Don Mig. Then will I dare possess it, father,
As talisman, an amulet of love,

An anchor to my soul, a charm to make
E'en better days for darling love and I,
To sweeten mine already sweetened love,
And make my dreams as beautiful as Cupids
Who wing their way in night-time o'er the couches
Of old new lords of love, till lovely Cadiz
Seems full of Spanish maids and brilliant ladies!
  Anso. Thou art full sick with love, Don Miguel;
And e'en thy waking evening hour is dream
To thee, since I am dead these hundred years!
  Don Mig. Dead? Anso, thou art riddle of the gods,
And, Ate-like, thou wouldst befuddle me
With hate and old revenge. But love tells true
Thou art no ghost, but ghost tho' thou mayst be;
Yet linger with thine Atlan story, since,
O Priest of Saturn, I have come to thee
With many a piteous tale; for love besets me
Upon three several sides.
  Anso.   I am a ghost;
But tell thine everlasting tale, since love
Hath thousand tongues, and stories sweetened rare,
And 's never done till lady sleepeth last
In marble tomb of unrelenting death;
But speak, Granada; love is never old.
  Don Mig. Upon three several sides I am beset:
Upon my wicked side, because my sword
I carry there, fair wild Gitano sits,
The dancing girl of Gades, with a skin
Olive, and eyes as dark as midnight skies,
A beggar beauty whose bright dagger, father,
Would cut my heart for unrequited love.
  Anso. A dangerous lass is this Moreno, Don;

Her race is treacherous.   Love her, all is well.
  Don Mig.   I love her as the gadfly or the jackdaw,
As cat the mouse, the boy the butterfly,
A prisoner his cell, a queen her throne.
  Anso.   Why riddle thus?   Thou lov'st her for the hour?
She is thy beer, but not thy luscious wine?
  Don Mig.   Yea, common as my beer, mine ancient sack ;
But Cousin Inez !   Ah, High Priest of Saturn,
She 's jewel-fashioned finely.   Born a beauty,
She yet sits on the north of my affections ;
Since though as lovely as a star, as pure,
I hate her ; for I 'm plighted by my father,
Her father.
  Anso.   'Tis love's old, old story, Don.
  Don Mig.   To keep the name of Santa Rosa, father,
Imperishable in the realm of Spain,
Don Pedro Santa Rosa de Granada,
Father of Inez, and mine old ambitious
Pa, touched their Spanish noses o'er their wine,
And plighted us for life, eternity ;
But little caring for this Inez, father.
Yet hear my story.   She was foolish eight,
And I sixteen, when o'er their Gascon wine
They plighted us.   Forsooth !   Two paltry knaves
Who only money had in winy thought.
I know she's fair as lilies of the valley,
As pure as Geyser waters, lucent wines,
That she is heiress to the Santa Rosa
Estates.
  Anso.   In case of her demise?
  Don Mig.   Then, father,
All Santa Rosa lands revert to me.

Anso. And thou dost marry her?

Don Mig. 'Tis but the same.
Yet, listen. Still another findeth place
Within my heart.

Anso. Thou hast a triple love?

Don Mig. Indeed! But out of such a brilliant three
I choose Dolores Castro! She is fair;
The glory of Seville; and can be had
Just for the winning.

Anso. Let me tell thee now,
Forever! Choose fair Inez for thy wife,
And all thine earthly troubles will be o'er.

Don Mig. Forbear, oh Priest of Saturn! Love will
guide.

Anso. Once married to Dolores, trouble, trouble.

Don Mig. But love is mine immortal counterpart.

Anso. Once wedded to the dark Moreno, life
Will be a farce or tragedy of old.

Don Mig. Believe me, Anso, thou art very ghost;
For I am sleeping here upon the public
Stage, aye! the world's great rostrum, where we actors
But do our unavoidable parts, and quick
Retire from life and hoary seeming death,
To turn to native dust, the food for worms
And all things vile. But, father, answer me,
What makest thou? 'Tis rare beyond compare,
And fills me with a kind of holiness.

Anso. Young man, I am the shade of other years;
Am resurrected from a past so distant,
It is forgot, and things of now seem strange
And wonderful. But since I'm here amid
Thy dreaming hours, I'll tell thee all my story.

I am the Priest of Saturn.   I am mighty
In spirituality.   Goodness is my business.
I lived when th' Trident was the symbol of
Atlantic, when the prows of all her vessels
Spread fame throughout the kingdoms of the world ;
Her colonies did flourish from Peru,
Central America, Spain, and Ireland, Egypt,
The Mediterranean, ay ! the then known world.
With knowledge strange, occult of hidden things,
I sought this Atlan opal, rare and fine :
To amulet in shape of human heart
I fashioned it, a gem, a rarity ;
And whoso doth possess it, hath protection
From Ate, Nemesis, and all bad gods.
    Don Mig.   But who so lucky as to gain its keeping ?
    Anso.   To him, who was a ruler o'er proud Gades,
My nephew, was the amulet presented.   (*Ex.* Anso.
    Don Mig. (*Aside.*)   St ! Mark ye, I, Granada, must
        possess it.
Now out upon thee as a priestly coward !
What !   Gone ?   And not a footfall ?   I alone ?
What means it ?   Were it gray old dawn of day,
I'd have the explanation in my wine-cups ;
But, lo !   'Tis only evening, and my head's
As clear as cowbell flower or buttercup
In daisied meads.   My three green loves, Dolores,
Moreno, and my cousin rare, have turned
My head ; I'm drunk with interlacing sweets ;
I'm dreaming, or 't 's hallucination strange.
No Priest of Saturn here ?   What doth it mean ?
'Tis strange, aye, strange.   It mimes with gaunt old meanings
And 's warning unto me in all my loves.

I'll hence to Santa Rosa's house, in Cadiz,
And he shall tell me of this new Atlantis.

        Enter PRINCE HENRIQUE.

    Henrique. Ha, ha! And fools do dream upon their
        legs,
Their eyes wide staring. Priest of Saturn! Ha,
My feathered lord, he's dead these thousand years.

    Don Mig. What villain clown is this? (*Drawing his
        sword.*)

    Henrique.   'Tis Prince
        Henrique!

    Don Mig. A prince? Forsooth!

    Henrique.   A prince, forsooth!

    Don Mig.   A
        coward!

    Henrique. Dost lose thy courtly temper?

    Don Mig.   Aye, false
        prince!

    Henrique. At home, and such a courtier lord as thou
Had tasted this late red Damascus blade.

    Don Mig. A quarrel's not for time nor place.

    Henrique.   Then
        cross!

    Don Mig. My basket-hilted sword is good as thine;
So, have a care, and guard thy treacherous heart;
And back, or I shall run thee through, petard!

    Henrique. Thy guard, Sir Boaster, or thy Spanish
        blood
Shall dye thy footing-place.

    Don Mig.   'Tis thine to win,
If so thou handle thy good sword. Come, prince!
(*They fence rapidly for a moment.* HENRIQUE *suddenly
            draws back.*

Henrique. Thou art a pretty swordsman.

Don Mig.   So art thou.

Henrique. Come, let's be friends; we seem of liker
metal;
And here's my hand.

Don Mig.   And mine in kindly token.

Henrique. Now tell me who thou art: because one man
Alone in Spain can wield the sword like thee.

Don Mig. His name?

Henrique.   Don Miguel de Santa Rosa
Granada.

Don Mig. 'Tis mine own name: and but one
Can face me, sire, as thou hast. 'Tis the son,
Plumed sirrah! of the Duke of old Medina—
Sidonia. Art thou he, a stranger here?

Henrique. I am; and we shall have no further quarrel
Until some gypsy maid divide her love.
But, hark. The Priest of Saturn was thy theme;
And wast thou fooling with thy courtly self?

Don Mig. Not I; for Anso walked these boards to-
night.
And only on your quick arrival went.

Henrique. Beneath the eaves I heard thy talk, and saw
No man, not e'en the semblance of a ghost;
And to myself I said: This man's a fool.
For he doth prate of love to hoary shadows;
He talks of dancing girls of wild Gitano
Blood.

Don Mig. Careful!

Henrique.   And of some Dolores fair.

Don Mig. My sword is itching for patrician blood.

Henrique. Thine easy angers may cost blood, and thine!

Don Mig. Defy me not, O false and foreign prince!

Henrique. And further in this rare delightful story,
We hear of Inez. To thine old guitarra
Dost sing: O wild Lolita?

Don Mig.   Dost thou toy?

Henrique. And then on softer strings, in cadence rare,
O, dear Dolores, fair Dolores.

Don Mig.   Scoundrel!

Henrique. And then a string to love, e'en pathos tuned:
Oh, fairest Inez, angels guard thy couch.

Don Mig. Hast come to Spain to lose thy foreign
   blood?

Henrique. And all thy loves were queen: Moreno
   wild;
Dolores fair, and Inez rare.

Don Mig.   Get hence,
Or draw!

Henrique. My sword? Nay, Cupid draws his courtier,
His blatant lord, and with a spider string
So fine, my Miguel deems he leads the battle.
Have done with such sweet folly, for 'twill sour thee;
Give sleepless nights, a lusty, fool-hard temper;
A spite for quarrels with a saucy style.

Don Mig. Sir, were I not so late in priestly presence,
A foreign prince had bit our Spanish dust.

Henrique. I've come not here to brew a Spanish
   quarrel;
My heart is love; my sword is love; my thought,
Come, come, Don Miguel, wilt share thy loves?
Let wild Lolita be my gypsy nymph.

Don Mig. Prince, take her; I've no quarrel for Moreno.

Henrique. Two loves are more than feast, e'en for a

lord ;
So, let the Donna Inez be my prize.

Don Mig.   When babes in years, our fathers plighted us.

Henrique.   Then even she shall be my wedless bride?

Don Mig.   A thousand yeses.   She's my cousin fair.

Henrique.   My titles, Miguel, are high as thine.

Don Mig.   No doubt can enter.

Henrique.   For the doors are shut.
But tell me, are we not well met?

Don Mig.   As courtiers?

Henrique.   And swordsmen of the finest ardor?

Don Mig.   Aye !

Henrique.   And so of every capon we must share
A leg.

Don Mig.   And half and half of wing and breast.

Henrique.   But thou shalt have the tail, for thou art last.

Don Mig.   I read thy sarcasm in thy words and manners ;
Yet dare resolve this riddle ; for my business
Doth draw me hard.

Henrique.   And e'en as hangman's rope.

Don Mig.   Hark, sirrah !   I have done with innuendoes.

Henrique.   Then draw, and briefest time shall settle it !

(*They commence action, when with a scream,* LOLITA MO-
RENO *springs between them.*

Lolita.   Oh, Miguel, don't lose thy life for such !

Henrique.   What jade is this?

Lolita.   A dancing girl of Spain !

Don Mig.   And I'll defend her with my life.   Aside !

Henrique.   Wilt draw thy sword for such a strumpet?

Lolita.   Yes !

Henrique.   Then faretheewell, my doughty hero.   Bye !

(*Ex.* HENRIQUE.

Lolita. And never cast thy shadows more in Spain.

Don Mig. Lolita, mind him not; my love for thee
Is boisterous as the brooks of Cadiz.

Lolita. Yes.

Don Mig. And ever shall my sword defend thee, darling.
Come, let me lead thee to this rustic seat,
And with mine old guitarra will we while ·
A passing hour, and in such songs to thee,
That dark Moreno's heart shall beat in tune;
And then the grave old saraband may dance.
There, my Gitano, what is this but loving?
If every courtier, duke or titled lord,
Should act his heart, the dancing girls of Spain
Would lead them to the altar. Now a dance,
And o'er the silk and silver strings I'll wander,
While featly thou wilt foot it like a sylph.

Lolita. Love's blind; but I will dance his old fandango.
　　(*Dances.*

Don Mig. Ha, that is fine as Moorish maid, Moreno.

Lolita. And does my dancing please Don Miguel?

Don Mig. Better than courtly lady, beauty fair.

Lolita. I'm gladdened if so great a lord is pleased.

Don Mig. Now sing with thy wild sweet voice, and
　　thy race
Will glory in thy loveliness, while I
Do drink thy rapturous beauty dark and rare.

Lolita. I dance for thee; I sing to thee, for love!
　　(*Sings.*

SONG.

A courtier knight, a Spanish lord, ·
　　Doth love Moreno fair,
And on the old guitarra, love,

We 'll sing her beauty rare.

CHORUS.

    Oh sing tra la,
      Oh sing tra lee,
    On old guitar,
    On old guitar,
      In love's med–lee.

Moreno is a dancing girl,
    The rarest of her kind,
She floats with airy pirouette,
    With magic of the wind.

CHO.

Her eyes are black, her skin is dark,
    Her soul is in her eyes,
Her beauty is the beauty, love,
    Of starry midnight skies.

CHO.

Don Mig. Thy song is beautiful as thine own self.

    (ALBERTI, *her gypsy lover, suddenly enters.*

Alberti. What hound is this? (*Yanking* MORENO *to her feet.*

                      Moreno, art thou mad?
Sir villain, draw thy sword, and skill shall tell !
Thy courtier blood is blue, but mine is red.
So, villain, draw !

    Lolita.   Alberti, back ! He 's master.

    Alberti.   Black wench, aside, or my Gitano blood
Shall vent its ire on thee !

    Don Mig.   Go pluck his sleeve,
And lead him from this amphitheatre ;
I 'd sob to shed his blood. Poor man, his love
Hath made him mad. And such a man as he ;

So tall, so dark, with raven, curly locks,
And whiskers like a pirate's. Lola, go !
His love is gold to mine of silver. Lead
The way. and never shall a lord dare sing
Another song of love on Spain's guitar
To airy dancing maid, Moreno Lola.

    Alberti. But, let me at the scoundrel, maid Gitano.

    Lolita. Alberti, have no word with him ; he's kind
To dancing girls like me. I'm sure his soul
Is pure. My love should pacify Alberti.

    Alberti. For once it shall ; but ere she lead me hence,
Bold knave, a word with thee. Once touch a hair
Of my Moreno's head, and young Granada's
Blood—But, I go. Moreno, lead me out. (*Ex. both.*

    Don Mig. A booby. Faugh ! I should have run him
        thro' ;
But, no—Poor fool, he loves her with his heart,
While I with touch of sensuality ;
I'd kill the dog should he molest me further.
But faugh ! I've bigger fish than such as he.
This foreign prince hath something of the rascal ;
And yet a kind of fascination. He
Doth puzzle me. 'Twere luck, since but for this,
Our quarrel had assumed a deadly ending.
(*He turns to pass out, when he is met by* INEZ, *who is in
    half mask.*

    Inez. Don Miguel ?

    Don Mig.   Yes, Inez, and thy lover.
But why dost come ? The hour is late, and scoundrels
Begin their wicked tramps. with darkness as
Disguise. A maid so delicate as thou
Should hie her home to mother's covering wing.

But, look!   Thou art disguised!   Why domino
On face so fair?   'Tis love and jealousy
Upon a rampage.   Pray, wilt tell thy lord?

    Inez.   Dost know a coarse Gitano dancing girl?

    Don Mig.   Ha, ha!   and so god Cupid leads my lassie?
Too good, too good!   Pray, Inez, let me dare
Remove thy domino;   for thou art passing
Fair;   lily beauty from some tropic clime:
A house-plant watered by the tears of lovers.   (*Removes mask.*
Thou art too fair;   and every noble eye
Will bear me out in't.   So, a dancing gypsy
Hath robbed my lady of her quiet.   Ha,
Love oft hath made a crown of thorns.   But, Inez,
Go rest in peace;   I'm true as Polar star;
My love is clear and pure as Polar night;
The glittering Polar stars his anadem.

    Inez.   I will confess my love for thee hath led
Me out, and in such hour that I do tremble.

    Don Mig.   But be no more aroused;   for such a love
As mine can guard thee all thy livelong days,
And make thy life a running ditty.   Come,
Let's forth.   But, stay;   a Peter for thy Paul.
Didst notice in thy nightly rambles, Prince
Henrique, dressed in faultless foreign garb,
With such emboldened air and iced exterior,
That frigid smiles did play across his features?

    Inez.   I met a courtly man as tall as thou,
With such degree of court politeness that—

    Don Mig.   That what?

    Inez.   He turned aside and circled
       round
Me, lifting such a hat of loveliness,

I could but change my courtly etiquette
With him.

Don Mig. Then will we toss a penny, love;
For, 'tween us is a bow, a Spanish song.
Fair Inez, are we not at quits? 'Tis so;
Lolita danced and sang for me; the prince,
Ha, doffed his hat and circled round thee so! (*Imitating.*

Inez. Restore my mask, and I will hie me hence
And nevermore go watching. Wilt forgive me?

Don Mig. And with a kiss, if stage propriety
Forbade it not. But thought is deed for such.
When marriage crowns us, and old Hymen lights
Us to our bridal couch, then shall our kisses
Re-echo to the night, and gossips hear
No echoings. But, let me be thy knight;
For clouds have curled across the sky, and stars
Twinkle behind impenetrable darkness,
The sad round moon illuming but in vain.

Inez. If other business call thee, night for me
Hath not a frighting harm. My love is brave.

Don Mig. (*Aside.*) 'Twill be a hero if in battle for
Granada's heart!

Inez. Wast speaking, Miguel?

Don Mig. One only thought, but thou wert in it, Inez.
But, come. I'll be thy starless night escort;
And dancing girl or prince durst cross our path,
I'll have the right of deadly arbitration!

Enter MIDDLE.

What knave of trumps is this? Our worthy clown.

Middle. They call me Middle. Why? The fool is in
The middle. But, now begging clownly pardons,
I just rubbed up against a courtly fool,

If fool can see a fool. Don Miguel.

    Don Mig.   What! cursed Henrique?   Fool!   Thy
     hand, fair Inez ;
Since I would lead thee from such paltry prince.
Old trouble goes a-brewing night and day,
And rises from the clown to lord or prince.   (*Leads her out.*

    Middle.   A fool by nature I, but he through love.
I sleep and dream because I know no better ;
They lie awake and dream because of love.
That I could be as wise as he for seconds,
To know just how a self-made fool doth feel.
Ah ! enters love's true pattern of a man,
And something near as pretty as a girl ;
And yet a man, a human, human man,
I'll get behind the wing, and fool-like listen
To life's dear love-made fool. One fool 't to time ;
Enter, my wise apportioned counterpart. (*Hides behind the
    wing. Enter* PRINCE HENRIQUE.

    Henrique.   Was never such a lovely maid in all
The realm of Spain. She raised her domino ;
But haply that I were some other lord ;
Perchance, this proud Granada. Ha, ha, ha !
A triple villain truly. Three strange loves ;
One, Lola, a Gitano dancing girl,
With such a midnight beauty, e'en old courtiers
Find their dull hearts a-pounding 'gainst their sides.
And Inez. For some old hidalgo gossips
Did prate the secrets of the town because,
Forsooth ! I am a master of the sword,
And hied me from a foreign land with suite
Of lovely gentlemen that beggar art.
What foolish men we women are. A hoax ?

I mean we men turned womanish by women.
Ha, ha, there's Miguel; a Spanish hero,
As brave as Cæsar; master of the sword;
A glorious good companion; wit and wine
His mottoes; ever ready at a need;
Sharing his last pistole; and yet I dub him
A pickaninny dressed to please the fair.
Out on a pickpurse lord like him. I'm tired
Seeing brave men still tied to ladies' skirts.
Ah! here's a maudlin fool; old nature did it.

Enter MIDDLE, *grinning.*

Well, well, thou leering ninny, why hast come?.

Middle. Because my legs would argue 'gainst my mind.

Henrique. Legs? Middle, poor are legs in argument.

Middle. A clownly pardon. But thou'lt hear a clown?

Henrique. A fool or clown, 'tis all the same to princes.

Middle. I stole a capon from the roosting.

Henrique.   Well.

Middle. My legs were wiser than a lord; they ran.

Henrique. And that was all thy lawyer's argument?

Middle. Nay; for I fed my legs down thro' my mouth.

Henrique. Devoured the chicken?

Middle.   Yea; and crowed
    for more.

Henrique. How so?

Middle.   The chicken was a rooster, sir.

Henrique. Thou art a fool indeed, a very fool.

Middle. But had Henrique my two legs, 'twere well.

Henrique. Pray tell me ere thy blood's upon my sword!

Middle. He would have run away from maid Dolores.

Henrique. But I do know her not. Explain, thou fool!

Middle. All men do bow to Queen Dolores, sir.

Henrique. And so must I needs take to paltry legs?

Middle. Yea; trust thy legs in love for all thy heart;
For legs in love have more of earthly wisdom.

Henrique. Don Miguel hath several loves, dear clown.

Middle. Then several times as big a fool as thou.

Henrique. And both his legs have failed to extricate
   him?
But hence! I'm fooling with my heart's true love:
And as the saying is: One fool't to time.

Middle. I go; but when did love e'er get along
Without his fool?

Enter INEZ.

Inez.   Dear Middle, who is this?

Middle. A man, if still he be a prince, Miss Inez.

Henrique. A thousand princely pardons, senorita.

Inez. Senor, I am intrusive; I'll withdraw.

Henrique. Thou hast such art and life's divinity,
No foreign lord could fail to bow to thee.

Enter DOLORES.

Dolores. And here are maidens fair and very fine;
But handsome gentlemen call me divine!

Henrique. O what a beauty of a woman, Inez.

Inez. Indeed, as lovely as a bridal rose.

Henrique. A Spanish lass—(*Enter* MIGUEL *suddenly,
   drawing his sword.*

Don Mig.   Ho! draw, thou paltry villain,
And Inez and Dolores be the judges!

Middle. I'll get my bandage; soon two bloods will flow.

Inez. Don Miguel, put up thy coward sword.

Henrique. Or mine shall spill thy treacherous blood,
   bold prince!

(*They fence. As* MIGUEL *falls from a thrust, into the arms*

of DOLORES, MORENO *rushes between them, wounded
by* MIGUEL'S *flying sword, but is caught in the arms
of* ALBERTI, INEZ *fainting and falling into the arms
of* HENRIQUE, *the clown staring in a corner.*

CURTAIN FALLS.

MY AIDENN

MY AIDENN.

Oh have you seen my castle?
　　Ah me! down by the sea;
My castle, tasseled castle,
　　And built so wondrously,
Built on a plan of beauty
　　Surpassing any dream,
My tessellated castle
　　With silver joist and beam?

A window facing heaven
　　Where brightest angels be,
My fairy, airy castle
　　Fronting the restless sea,
Aye restless when I'm sleeping,
　　Sleeping my sleep of love,
With sands and waters round me,
　　And eve's one star above.

For architect a Cupid
　　With newly-fledgèd wing,
So beauty, beauty, beauty,
　　And I the crownèd king!
A king in such a kingdom,
　　I'm happy at the thought,
I'm happy in this kingdom,
　　There is no happier spot!

I have a priceless Raphael,
  Raphael and Keats and Keats,
I have all kinds of music,
  A nook with rustic seats,
Cupids in silver fountains,
  And o'er my fabric whole,
And o'er my glorious fabric
  The beauty of the soul.

The sea-mew moaneth, crieth,
  Crieth for joy all day,
In undertone the breakers
  Moan out a roundelay,
Moan out, and yet a ditty
  As soft as sigh or kiss,
It seems to me, it seemeth
  Here in this vale of bliss.

New veiny shells and pebbles
  Washed by a thousand waves,
A thousand waves in trebles,
  In little bars and staves,
Roll at my feet, and to them
  I say: "O ocean shell
And pebble, what's your mission,
  A kiss or faretheewell?"

I fondle ; unreplying,
  They shine and sparkle so,
Sparkle and shine so wondrous,
  Oh be it yea or no?
Yea, shall I fondle, linger?
  Since in my dreams with thee,
I hear a far off music
  Intonèd by the sea.

Is't love ?   I'm not so foolish ;
    My castle !   Ah, too true,
No maiden fair or elfish
    Shall dare dispute with you ;
For, hear me, stone and mortar,
    Mortar and groinèd stone,
My castle's for a hermit,
    I'd live here all alone.

A skiff, a boat so dainty
    'Twould tip with Cupid in,
A lullaby is playing :
    "We have no kith and kin !"
And so I'm free as breakers,
    Breakers with crests of foam,
That sparkle, flash and shimmer
    Around my castle home.

Around my castle lordly,—
    And O the peace to me !
And O the music in me !
    The music of the sea ;
So glorious, olden, golden,
    My castle wondrous fair,
So olden, golden, glorious,
    Divinity is there !

Architrave and rafter,
    Rafter and lintel too,
The corbel old, fantastic,
    No mortal more could do :
Demoniac spirits come not,
    Demoniac elfs are far,
The beauty that is o'er me
    Is made of moon and star.

I dine with rosy nectar
  Winking with bubbly eyes.
Ah me! I have ambrosia,
  And wines from sunny skies:
I brim my beakers, beakers,
  My beakers lined with gold,
The wine I quaff's delicious,
  Delicious in cobwebs old.

I fondle Poe in visions,
  In visions with him lie,
Our only golden poet!
  Our only? Tell me why?
Verlaine in rhythmic numbers,
  With haunting melodies,
Weird melodies fantastic,
  Sad, sombre, elfish glees.

With rapturous, beauteous music,
  Yea, beauteous, too, as death,
When new love's loveliest maiden—
  Hush! giveth up her breath!
With cadence dripping glorious
  The red, red wines of thought,
With heaven and hell contending
  In beauties he has wrought.

And so the wingèd sunshine
  Chases the shadows grim,
Chases from nook and corner,
  Till wraiths, ah, faint and slim,
As apparitions, haunt me,
  Spirits of those I knew;
But, O delicious, luscious,
  To be with such as you!

Against my window, music,
  Fantastic, half divine,
Divine and heavenly wondrous,
  Sparkling like beaded wine,
White wine that makes capricious
  Dream-fancies unto me,
Until I laugh ecstatic,
  Demoniac in my glee.

Taine, Lamb, Montaigne and Zangwill,
  Yea, glorious are to me,
The friends I love, the friendships
  Best for their rarity!
As scarce as Brownings, Shelleys,
  A Coleridge, yea, a Poe;
But well-a-way, I'm happy,—
  The sea-wave boometh low.

The sea-wave is my organ,
  My emerald minstrelsy,
In undertone majestic,
  In horrid revelry;
In cadent, rhythmic numbers,
  Diversified for me,
Come o'er me, to me, to me,
  These ballads of the sea.

So, here I'd live forever,
  Forever, yea and aye,
With nothing diabolic,
  Nothing to slay or flay;
Great ships with sails outbellied,
  White glistening on the wave,
White glistening like a phantom,
  Sail on with runic stave.

And I am left forever
  In castle by the sea,
With organ tones majestic,
  Buried in majesty,
Buried in hoary glories,
  Glories of wind and wave,
And should I die angelic,
  Let ocean be my grave!

SONG OF THE SEA SHELL

SONG OF THE SEA SHELL

Through diamond sands I wander
  In olden glories lost,
In old fantastic beauties,
  Holding a shell embossed
With many a wavy nodule,
  A message-shell to mé,
A message from the ages,
  And tell-tales of the sea.

I sit me wayward, curious,
  Curious in phantasy,
O'erfilled with revelations,
  And love-songs of the sea.
And love-songs, ditties olden.
  Olden like corkèd wine,
The wine of tipsy Bacchus,
  Reveling with maids divine.

And as I sit, my sea-shell
  Telleth a tale to me,
A song, a song, a love-song.
  The mystery of the sea ;
A song so weird, so elfish,
  Elfish and weird and fine,
I clasp it for its glory,
  Its tell-tales of the brine.

I kiss it, who may know it?
   Perchance a mermaid queen.
With rapturous kiss ecstatic,
   Kissed it in ocean's green :
Yea, kissed it with a passion,
   A passion mermaids know,
Down, down in ocean kingdoms,
   Where moon-tides ebb and flow.

Where mermen, mermaids wander
   In ocean jubilee,
Shells, carcanet, fantastic,
   And rare festivity ;
Where grottoed reefs of coral,
   Corals by insects built,
Sparkle and shimmer, sparkle
   Like diamonds on a hilt.

So, tell me, ocean, ocean,
   So, tell me, empty shell,
What secret hast thou, hast thou?
   What secret hast to tell?
I hold you, and I hear you,
   Singing a song, a song,
Who made your ocean music
   That singeth all day long?

I found you on the seashore
   Buried in sifting sand,
Oh did you hie from India?
   Or is't your native strand?
A weird hallucination,
   Fantastic as a dream,
Haunteth my soul, O Sea-shell!
   With evanescent gleam.

Did ocean queen e'er string you,
  And play old roundelays?
Rondels of cavallieros,
  In olden, golden days?
What pearls have heard your music?
  Your song is never old,
A thousand years 'twill murmur
  To ages yet untold.

And yet I cannot solve you,
  Your song is hid from me.
Within your minstrel bosom
  Is hid your melody ;
Your song is never ending,—
  What other age shall hear?
O will you e'er be voiceless,
  And silent to the ear?

HELL AND HEAVEN

HELL AND HEAVEN

They drag me hellward, mother,
  They drag me hellward aye,
They drag me hellward, hellward,
  They drag me though I pray;
I see them idiotic,—
  O how their red eyes gleam!
Their power, oh 'tis despotic,
  They seize me in my dream!

I try to shape and fashion
  A manner of escape,
But devils diabolic,
  They mime and stare and gape,
Till beads of perspiration
  Rush startled to my face,
O horrid, weird damnation
  Translate me from this place.

But, nay, the crownèd goblet
  Is pressèd to my lip,
"Taste, mortal, weary mortal,
  Yea, take a human sip!"
But, nay, I dash it from me,
  I see the shattered glass;
"Get hence, uncertain shadows,
  I go to holy mass!"

But, Mother Mary, mother,
   Good angels kiss my brow,
Kiss me, angelic, rapturous,
   And 'tice me heavenward now:
Their white wings fan my curtains,
   An odor comes to me,
As from a swinging censer
   Hung in eternity!

"O how the music playeth!—
   They bear me to the sky,—
Oh let me dream in odors,
   In dreamland let me lie."
"But, nay, you conquered, mortal,
   The miming devils lost;
Your dream will end in heaven,
   You won at any cost!"

So, hell and heaven's contention,
   Mangled, but left me free,
As wingèd bird in ether,
   As sea-mew o'er the sea;
As bee on swinging floweret,
   A pure, a perfect whole,
And 'spite of hell, demonian,
   Heaven won a perfect soul!

AMABEL

AMABEL

Her eyes were as the star-shine.
　　When skies are blue, so blue,
Amabilis, my love-queen,—
　　O for a world like you!

I love you, love you, love you,
　　Amabilis, my Bel,
Down deeply in my bosom,
　　Deeper adown than hell!

All night-time in my spirit,
　　When clouds go hide and seek,
With her I go; seraphic,—
　　She loves me if she speak;

But when the veils of morning
　　By angels are withdrawn,
By angels, holy angels,
　　My idol maid is gone!

Last e'en I saw an angel,
　　But now I go to her;—
I start and stare theatric!—
　　Must love drink myrrh, love's myrrh?

Love's aberration, ' ation, .
  Is in her lovely eye ;
My God, my God, my Jesus,
  Drop mercy from the sky !

"My Amabel, a demon,
  A demon wicked, fell,
Has ta'en your reason, reason,
  My spotless Amabel !

"Oh horrid aberration ! .
  So wicked, cruel, fell,
You've ta'en her perfect reason,
  Amabilis, my Bel !"

Oh eyes ! oh where your meaning?
  Where love in loveliness?—
Now waits hallucination
  To kill Amabilis ;

To kill where love made beauty,
  A beauty love could see ;
But, ah ! this dissolution,
  The living death to me !

I try to win love-glances,
  The poem of her face,
The poem only love's eyes
  In love can fondly trace :

Ah me ! I'm but a stranger,—
  What made her love me so,
And then with toppling reason,
  Turn eyes that do not know?

I take her hand; ecstatic,
  I fondle and caress,
I touch her lips with kisses,—
  She stares. O my distress!

I show the old love fondness;
  I cry: "My Amabel!"
Her love has said: " 'Tis over;
  It is our last farewell!"

Then reason made her beauty?—
  As marble is she fair!
A Greek Slave in her beauty,
  But life is wanting there!

Her eye is unresponsive,
  Her cheek?—the rose is gone;
Oh great world, you are empty,
  Though you may jangle on!

Come back in marble whiteness,
  O soul of Amabel,
Come back to love's dear palace,
  Come back, forever dwell

In love's dear tabanacle,
  In love's cathedral home;
For where a lovelier prison?
  Come back, white soul! don't roam.

But sackcloth, dust and ashes,
  Her eye will shine no more;
Her eye, her face are vacant,
  Vacant forevermore;

So, what is love?   Who knoweth?
  She loved, but now loves not:
I am a perfect stranger,—
  My love she has forgot!

So, to my love's dominion
  Came imps of horrid dread.
Came to my love's dominion,
  Till Amabel lies dead!

Yea, dead to love and loving,
  And dead to even me;
So, faretheewell, my darling,
  Love's last farewell to thee!

FINIS.

www.ingramcontent.com/pod-product-compliance
Lightning Source LLC
Chambersburg PA
CBHW020751020726
47495CB00008B/2382